GODS OF OUR TIME

A Paris Love Story

Michael Bowker

Library of Congress Cataloging-in-Publication Data is available

Michael Bowker

Gods of Our Time: A Paris Love Story/ by Michael Bowker – 1st ed.

p. cm.

1. Romance – Paris – Fiction. 2. Adult Love Story – Paris – Popular Fiction. 3. Historical Romance – Personal Discovery – Fiction. 4. 1920s Paris – Interpersonal Relationships – Fiction.

ISBN   978-1-7334321-9-1

eBook ISBN 978-1-7334321-8-4

To my beautiful and
talented daughters,
Kristine and Michele.

ACKNOWLEDGEMENTS

To my friends and family I owe such a debt for the joy they still bring to me every day. I loved every morning I sat down to write this book, and many people were part of that. Besides my lovely and supportive daughters, Michele and Kristine, I want to especially thank Colleen Gilliam, for her superb editing and steadfast encouragement over the past few years. It remains essential to me.

I also want to thank Yuliya Lennon, who not only painted the fantastic cover for this book, she read it thoroughly and gave me vital suggestions. Yuliya, born in Russia and educated in London, has a PhD in linguistics and is a brilliant artist. She is a member of the highly-respected Painter-Stainers Guild of London, one of the royal guilds in England. The first time I saw her paintings displayed, I was amazed at how much they reminded me of the feelings I was trying to capture in this book. I remain a huge fan of her work, some of which you can see at *www.Yuliyalennon.com*.

Special thanks is due to Cyndi Wells, with whom I've worked for many years on many books. She is one of the world's great graphic designers. Hopefully, we have many more projects ahead.

Many other people touched this book along the way, and it wouldn't have been the same without them. I owe a great debt to Daniel Dias, as well as Masha Malka, Maru Johansen, Nina Anderson, Frank Gaynor, Dannielle Merlino, Michelle Deen and many others for their support and suggestions.

I was also greatly encouraged by the kind words from Uri Singer, CEO of Passage Pictures.

Finally, I have my mother, Ellyn Larsen, to thank for just about everything, including her belief that anything is possible in this life. My sister, Sharon, also played an encouraging role in all of this. This book was written in memory of my father, who read to me every night when I was a child. I can still hear his kind voice.

I relied on many literary sources to get the setting and feel of Paris in the 1920s, but nothing prepared me as much as walking the boulevards and over the bridges and exploring the parks, cafes and back streets so many times. Each time was like the first.

PROLOGUE

Several months before she died, Sophie was curled up on the soft, blue couch in our living room, in the log home we loved on the north shore of Lake Tahoe.

The sunlight slanted through the big window and backlit her hair in a million silver sparkles. She looked like an angel. I ached to touch her, and I was taken by a desire to win her all over again. We had been married for more than five decades, but maybe all lovers feel that way, sometimes.

She had been thinking quietly for several moments. I could tell when something was going on in her mind. It was always worth waiting to see what it was. Outside, the aspen trees and the lake shimmered in the sunlight.

When I looked back, she was looking at me.

"You shouldn't start the book at the point where we first met," she said slowly. "You should start it when you and Margaret first went to Paris. If she hadn't done that ghastly thing, we might not have ever met."

I tried to absorb what she was saying, but I couldn't help being distracted by how beautiful she was.

"Jake!" she said.

I took two quick steps, kissed her lips, face, and hair; gave her a squeezing hug that made her gasp, and then quickly sat back down.

"Yes?" I asked.

She shook her head at me and looked away. I had a feeling she was smiling.

"More people will understand your story better than mine, so it should be written in first-person, from your point of view," she said. "Besides, you know your story. You can't know all of mine because you don't know how I felt at every moment."

I thought about that for a second, and then pulled a quarter out of my jeans.

"I'll flip you for it."

"Jake."

"It's the only way."

"No!"

"Call it."

"No!"

"Call it!"

"Heads!"

The coin flipped through the air and landed in my palm. I slapped it on my wrist and dramatically revealed it.

"Heads!" She laughed.

"I was going to write it that way, anyway."

She smiled triumphantly and came over to kiss me. Her laughter always cascaded in a rhythm, like a mountain stream over stones. I heard it every day in my head when I wrote these pages.

I could still pick her up, and I carried her into the bedroom.

"Just like Paris," she said.

"Only this time it will work out better."

"Prove it," she said.

I spent the rest of the afternoon proving it, and she said I succeeded.

That was, more or less, how this book began. She insisted I write it because it would keep us together for a little while longer. She was wrong. We will always be together in my mind.

I loved her, and I love her still.

Chapter 1

Paris, France, 1925

The first time I entered Paris, fog covered the city.

"I can't see a thing," I said.

"It doesn't matter," Margaret said. She was looking out the window, dressed in white, exquisite and untouchable.

I thought it mattered, but I didn't say anything.

I heard the city, though, which helped. It sounded perfect, as I'd thought it might. The iron shoes of horses moving on the sides of the boulevard made a fine noise on the cobblestones. I rolled the window down and heard soft French voices from the cafés and along the sidewalks. I think I fell in love with Paris then.

Margaret shivered. "Would you mind shutting the window?"

I did. I touched her arm, and she smiled, laid her hand on mine for a moment, and then withdrew it.

The hotel was small but clean. The concierge was a big, red-faced man with a bushy mustache and big, meaty hands that easily handled our luggage.

"*Bonsoir,*" he said, openly admiring my companion and nodding at me. "You are from the American magazine, no?" he added, his English understandable.

I nodded.

He smiled and hustled our bags—one for me and four for her—to a long, burnished wooden counter that I knew was hundreds of years old—older than New York.

"Two rooms?" he said, frowning with French disappointment.

"*Oui,*" I said. I had a sudden feeling that I should apologize, even though the second room was for another couple from the magazine. It was as if the burly concierge already sensed what was coming. The French.

The room was like the hotel: small, well organized and old. We were purposefully on the Left Bank. It was where *they* all were, and it was them I had come to find. I would have to search them out—I knew that—but it was okay with me. I wouldn't have been comfortable any other way.

From the window, I could just see the black, flat surface of the Seine River running quietly under the foggy lights of the heavy bridges. I knew from the maps that farther down, the chiseled gargoyles, saints, kings and chimeras clinging to the steep purchases of the Cathedral Notre-Dame would be visible when the fog lifted. Long ago, before the rain and fog washed it all away, the twin stone towers were vivid with color; now they rose gray and stained in the fog and rain. The cathedral once had been described as France's most terrible church, but I didn't think of it that way. I was anxious for the morning.

The bed was small, but since sleeping with Margaret was a lot like being in the army anyway, it didn't matter.

Margaret was beautiful, passionate and methodical. For her, making love was something to be done with precision; creativity made her nervous. Her body was well shaped, and the heat and glow of her satin skin and the geometrically perfect lines of her face rendered a thousand New York hearts. She was elegant, educated, and enigmatic. I was lost for her. I didn't mind the small bed.

When I woke in the morning, I came out from under the sheets and blanket fast. Margaret slept as I went to the window. It was Paris all right. The French morning was already underway. Rue Mouffetard cut in a lovely arc below the window. The buildings facing our small hotel on the other side of the street loomed above our room, their slanted, stilted roof angles reminding me of the hats of Napoleon's soldiers.

Below, on the narrow street, Parisians and American and British expatriates walked past the cafés and restaurants that alternated between market stalls piled high with bright vegetables and round, fat fruit. There were iced shellfish and meats. This had been the ancient road to Italy centuries before. Two young women in hats picked over a wooden box filled with dark red berries, and a man, big and American, bought chestnuts and oranges. He looked somehow familiar. He placed them in papers, put them in his bag and moved on, his gait slightly uneven but strong. The women remained, graceful and laughing to each other. They were soon joined by others shopping the market stalls. I was happy. It was 1925, and I was in Paris on dual assignments from the *Kansas City Star* and *Scribner's Magazine*. A perfect woman slept in my bed, and the sun was burning away the last of the night's fog.

Margaret and I had met nearly six months before in New York. I was there to accept a journalism award I had won for a series of stories I did for the *Star* exposing some rather nasty, unhealthy procedures being used by a few meat-packing plants in Kansas City and St. Louis. It was the same kind of thing Upton Sinclair had written about with great inspiration. A smart-ass critic had written that my writing style was "based more on perspiration than inspiration" but I had gotten things changed at the meat-packing plants, and I was working on the inspiration part. The award was the biggest reason I was there. Margaret's father was one of the senior editors for *Scribner's*, which was one of the sponsors of the national journalism awards. I did not know then what he had done to Margaret's mother or to Margaret herself. In public, he was a seemingly decent and professional man. All I knew at the time was that he liked what I had done, and he invited me out to a large dinner event, where I found myself seated next to Margaret.

She was dazzling; pearls, white opera gloves, hair swept up, and a floor-length beaded burgundy dress that clung to her long, graceful and exciting legs and—well, I don't remember much past that, except she also had the unsettling green eyes of a cat.

She was gracious, allowing me to be the center of attention, even though it was clear she had much more firepower in that getup than I did as I stood there holding my award. But she seemed to be happy sitting there with me. We talked, drank champagne and danced to the orchestra until they started putting the tables and chairs away. She leaned into me fully, and I kissed her on her full, expectant mouth before she climbed into her carriage.

"I'll expect a call," she said, turning inside the carriage. Her eyes were fixed on me.

"Of course," I said automatically, already knowing that

any more creative response would cause those cat eyes to narrow.

With a shout from the driver, the horses were off, she was off and six months later, we were off – to Paris.

We saw each other several times before Paris, though, while I was still in New York, and each time, I got a warm reception. Her father seemed impressed with my work, and I with the ardency of her embraces. We hit the jazz clubs, and once, we ducked into a speakeasy where a gangster-looking doorman let us in. She had gin and I had bourbon. We danced to the pinging rhythms of the jazz band, and people actually clapped for us at the end—for her anyway. She was all jazz and cool, sensual perfection. By the end of the week, I was in total infatuation, the dangerous kind.

We made love for the first time in New York. A big clock tower stood outside the window of the hotel like a sentinel, and somehow, it made me uncomfortable that first time. When you make love, you don't want to be reminded of what time it is.

I reluctantly went back to Kansas City and dragged myself into the *Star* office every day, and every day I wired her. For a time, my wires were witty and full of references to things we had done and touches I still felt on my skin, and the time her father gave us a fresh manuscript from a writer who had become one of the American literary comets in Paris, and we sat together in front of the fireplace and went over it, and marveled at the shorter, more powerful sentence structure. I wondered if I could ever write like that. I thought I could.

But after a time, I simply wrote to her, "I miss you awfully," and that was all I could find. Then, one freezing day in January, she wired that her father had continued to take an interest in my work and asked if I would take an assignment for *Scribner's Magazine*. It was the Paris assignment. I was to write a contemporary piece on the American writers and a few other artists who had accumulated there. I never told Margaret, but when I first received her wire, I ran around the newsroom, whooping and shouting like a man who had lost his mind, and then I ran out onto Vine Street into what had become a genuine Kansas snowstorm and continued to shout, clutching the wire in my fist high overhead, as I slipped and slid down the block.

"Are all writers crazy?" a voice shouted at me.

I looked over and saw it was a policeman I knew, standing on the side of the snowy street, shaking his head and grinning. He was a friend of my father's and we drank beer together sometimes when he was off duty.

"Paris, Tom!" I shouted. "I'm going to Paris!"

"Sure you are, Jakey-boy! Me too! Right after I get back from Istanbul and Timbuctoo. No more beer for you today!" He shook his head, laughed and moved up a side street.

I paid no attention to him. I was wild with it. I did not know Paris then, but I did know of many of the writers and artists who had gathered there. My father had read many of their books to me when I was young. They had attained a stature and nobility in his mind, and in my own, that was part magic and part myth. They were greater than aristocracy, their work sacred and beyond mortal hands or hearts. Their thoughts and words surely must come from a perfect place. They were the gods of our time.

There was a knock on the door. Margaret stirred but didn't open her eyes. I jumped over the edge of the bed, hot with Paris, crazy for the scent of fresh-baked bread that came up through the window. I opened the door, and the bull-like bellman was there. He immediately moved his head around mine to look into the room, searching surely for a glimpse of the sultry mademoiselle—my mademoiselle—perhaps still in night clothing. I had boxed in college and I felt like belting him one, but I took a breath, remembering this was Paris, not Kansas City. A city of love, art and romance, not battle.

Still.

"Do you wish coffee, breakfast, or perhaps a taxi?" he asked.

"No," I said. "We want to visit the cafés. We will walk today."

He shrugged. "Suit yourself." Then he stepped back and smiled at me. It was a genuine smile and even warm for a moment. That was the way the French were, I learned. *"Bienvenue a' Paris!"* he said.

Margaret slept through the baking-bread smell. I sat in a chair and watched her sleep. In one department, Margaret reminded me of my father. Margaret was a heart-stealing, refined beauty, like something you would see behind glass at an art museum, and my father, who farmed some river-bottom land during summers, often came home to dinner covered in mud, but there was a harmony of great expectations between them. The furrows of our farm were arrow-straight, dug just so deep, each seed planted an equal distance from the others. He was precise in his science, his rows of corn, and the perfection he demanded of me. I had always clung to the sheer wall of those expectations by my fingertips.

She woke. "Is there coffee?" she asked.

"I thought we'd go out to one of the cafés."

"I'd like coffee."

"All right, sure."

I went downstairs to the small hotel kitchen and poured a cup of coffee, careful to mix in one lump of sugar and a half-shot of cream just so. Thankfully, the bellman was nowhere in sight.

She inspected the cup and then took a small sip. No reaction. I waited. After a moment and a few more sips, she languidly opened her arms and beckoned me in. The silk of her blonde hair slipped over part of her face.

"We're in Paris," she said in a half giggle. "I think it is fine."

"It's perfect," I said.

She pulled me down and I kissed her lips softly. She pulled me in and kissed me hard.

"Do you have to work today?" She moved away and reached for her hairbrush.

I took a breath. It wasn't easy for me to let go just like that. I moved to a chair. "No, the first interview isn't until tomorrow."

"Good!" she said. "We can spend the day together in the city. I hope it isn't too cold."

Chapter 2

Outside the door the wind curled down the street at us with a noisy rush.

"Isn't this fantastic?" I shouted into the wind.

Margaret just shivered down against it. I moved us across the cobblestones to the sunny side of the street.

I felt as if I were flying. My heart was pounding, I tried to act calm and sophisticated, but I wasn't doing a good job of it. I was walking through history and I'd always had trouble containing my enthusiasm for history.

"Look at that!" I said, but Margaret was cold and didn't lift her head. Even when the sun rose up over the tops of the buildings that loomed over us on the narrow, twisting street, it didn't immediately warm her.

She leaned against me not saying anything, until we reached le Mouff, the open-air market, where the street suddenly came alive. It spilled over with Parisians and others from Europe, America and elsewhere. People came in from the side streets and the live, joyous, amoebic, moving mass milled into the market. It was so tight moving forward required strategy and patience. The sound of human voices, haggling over the price of plums, and engaging in meetings of friends, goodbyes, flirtations, and everything in-between rose up and swirled around us until it seemed as if all of Paris was in the market, and everyone had something to say.

Huge piles of leafy vegetables were stacked up, and berries, oranges and yellow plums spread across the stalls. The thick burgundy raspberries stood out and a woman smiled and gave Margaret and me a handful. We ate them with juice spilling over our fingers. There were barrels with iced crabs, oysters, shrimp and escargot on top. Other barrels lined the sides of the street, full of wine, headed for the night restaurants throughout the city. Rabbits hung beside the other meats and Margaret did not like them hanging like that.

"Where are we meeting Robert and Allison?" she asked, stepping quickly past the rabbits and out of the markets. Restaurants and bistros with awnings and chairs and tables took over from the product stalls on each side of the street.

"We'll see them this afternoon. Rather looking forward to it."

"Of course, Robert knows Paris. He lived here for years before moving to New York to work for my father."

"He knows these artists."

"Yes, he has lived all over the Left Bank. I know he used to drink with them, and they always talked about books and art and women, I suppose."

"Of course," I laughed. "Nobody talks more about women and knows less about them than writers."

"What don't you know about me?" Margaret asked, leaning away from me.

"Probably everything," I said, knowing immediately

it was the wrong thing to say. Margaret dropped her arm from mine. My response was not something a man should have said. To Margaret anyway, it meant I wasn't paying attention. I was trying to be humble, but I was to learn that men must apply humility carefully when they are with women. Excess often wrecked the effort.

"I know one true thing, you are beautiful."

That comment was met with a brief frown, but I knew I had just moved out of the basement.

"You know things about me," she persisted. "I wish you would tell them."

At the time, I had no idea she was reaching out. I doubt she knew it either, not consciously anyway. Her father was the oppressor and her mother, the victim, retreated from that oppression and then from life, increasingly sipping her lemon and gins. Margaret spent her time in the house trying to avoid her father's criticisms and helping her mother, who was rapidly becoming a ghost. She trusted only her own ability to survive. In those days, the latency of the damage done in childhood was something not yet talked about, so Margaret and I did the best we could in Paris that spring.

"You are perfect." I couldn't find the words to say more. I felt sick to my stomach. I was so far from perfect. "I'll tell you more when I'm better."

She was quiet, walking next to me, not touching me any longer. "You should tell me now."

"I don't want to get it wrong."

"Oh Jake," she sighed. "You just did."

I didn't like that feeling and walked on, not knowing what to say. She moved up, and we walked on together, but apart. The street smelled strangely of fall, of dried leaves and decay, but there was a strange energy in it, too, one that rode in on the wind. It was a deeper scent of leather, spice, and red wine aging in oak barrels. It made me feel better.

After a little while, Margaret sighed again and took my arm.

"Robert will help you get ready for tomorrow. He knows these writers and the artists, and he can fill you in."

"Yes, it will be all right," I said. "Being in Paris makes it all right."

That was a bit dramatic, maybe, but I really felt that way. As I finished speaking, two things happened at once. Directly in front of us, a small dark-haired man, in dark pants, shirt and jacket, appeared to bump deliberately into a couple who looked like tourists. They were about twenty feet away from us. The collision caused the tourists to stumble. As they did, I saw the small man reach deftly into the jacket pocket of the male tourist and pull out his wallet. I was about to shout and bolt forward when a deafening screeching noise struck us from behind. I turned in time to see a black dog get hit by a careening car that was now heading right for us. I grabbed Margaret and tumbled her to the side as the car roared by us, hit the high curb, tilted, and then slid on its side.

"Oh my God!" Margaret gasped.

The car came to a shuddering stop with two wheels spinning in the air. The small pickpocket was already there, running around the steaming engine and yanking open the driver's door. As I ran toward the car, the thief helped the driver out and led him to the sidewalk. Before

I could reach him, the pickpocket set the driver down on the sidewalk and looking back at me, ran to the dog, which was spinning in pain on the hard cobblestones. I could see blood on its fur and on the street. Without stopping, the thief scooped up the dog in both arms and disappeared down a dark side street. I was stunned by the quickness of it all, but I thought my best play was to help the driver, who was holding his head and moaning on the sidewalk.

"Never saw the animal until it was too late," he said to me, shaking his head.

"Damn dog! Damn animal. Is it all right?"

"Yes. Are you?"

He nodded. He felt his arms and legs and ran a hand over his stomach and shoulders. He shrugged. "I am not hurt," he said in accented English. "But a devil of a morning. Can you help, please, with the car?"

With the help of three other men, two Frenchmen and a red-headed Russian, who had wide, green trousers and a gap-toothed smile, we pushed the car over. It landed on its wheels and bounced, and then it sat there, ready to go, as if nothing had happened. It was scratched in places, but the engine fired up when the driver turned the key and he shrugged and put it into drive. He shifted into low gear and drove off slowly, waving and shouting "Merci!" several times. The Russian let out a whoop when the car drove away, but otherwise, nobody on the street paid much more attention to us. I grinned and gave a short wave to the Russian and the two Frenchmen. Then I walked quickly back to Margaret, who was standing on the sidewalk, away from the street. The two tourists, unaware of anything else that had happened, had left the square. Later, the man would wonder where he had left his wallet. There was nothing much I could do, and Margaret put her arm in mine and pulled me down the street.

"Well, that was certainly exciting," she said.

"I hope the dog is okay."

"I am glad you are okay," Margaret said, giving me a hug and putting her head to my chest. "Come on, though. We are late."

For a moment, I thought I saw a dark figure move around a far corner of the street and duck between the buildings. I couldn't have known then that the little thief was to play a huge role in all of our lives and that, for me, he would become the most dangerous man in Paris.

Chapter 3

As the participants of those events moved away from the intersection and traffic started up again, a dove arced overhead. It was white, and it flew directly over the man carrying the injured dog and kept going until it caught a river-bank thermal and glided into the light over the Luxembourg Gardens. Then it steeped up again and flew over a bearded man orating in front of a small crowd about the "hearts of men" and how the collective state was the heart of man. He shouted and beckoned to the crowd with his hands. "Comrades, come with me, give up your selfish seeking of material wealth. Let us join together as one for the communal good." Then he opened his arms and delivered his final line. "The day of the individual has passed!"

Many people, especially the young men in the crowd, cheered wildly at that. Others muttered and wandered away. By the time the police came by arrested the bearded communist, and took him away, the dove had flown north across the river again. It banked over the happy traffic, pedestrians, peddlers and gypsies of the Champs-Elysees. When it reached the top of a certain high-angled rooftop, the white dove flared its wings like Pegasus, tucked its head and fluttered downward. It landed softly, shook its wings out once, and then folded them and settled in.

The building below was a hospital of sorts. It was small, and people came there who were afflicted by special kinds of sickness. Many had been through the fighting and dying of World War I and they had come out the other side a little different. They were not able to fully get over the artillery blasting, terror and killings, so they came to escape and try to heal. Others were there too, and many of their wounds were not entirely physical. In many ways, it was an exceptional experimental ground for the doctors. Sometimes their patients healed, though, and never came back to the hospital.

One of the biggest reasons for the healing was a young woman, who worked inside the hospital. Had she been, by another chance, born anywhere outside the civilized Western World, she might have been revered as a shaman, healer, witchdoctor, or druid. She would have been seen to have magical powers of healing that were mystical and unexplainable. But, here, where science ruled, and medical men scoffed at those other things, she was known as a nurse and wore a crepe paper hat.

She seemed nonetheless happy with her work, and content to apply her remarkable abilities to those who needed her help. She was trim and fit and had dark hair. There was an aquiline and pleasing curve to her face and chin, but most striking were her startlingly big, dark blue-green eyes, which landed softly upon her patients with the grace of the dove on the roof. Sometimes, when she was determined, her eyes turned a smoky indigo with sparkles of light, and that was when it was time to listen and do what she said.

There was something of a purpose and sureness about her that made her patients feel safe and good, as though the day was going to take a good turn somewhere. It was an internal feeling, and the patients she tended to didn't know exactly why they felt that way, but she had that effect on almost everybody. She did not flirt with the men but kept a distance in a way that pretty women did without injuring a man. When asked if she "had someone," she would smile, shake her head and say, "I have all of you!"

Sophie told few people about her past. Most of her patients assumed that such a gentle person had a gentle past, but that was not true. She had grown up in the small French town of Flers, which suffered some of the fiercest bombings and fighting in the war. More than sixty thousand soldiers had died in the first few days of fighting within miles of her village.

The battle there had raged for six months, with more than one million casualties mounting up on both sides. Afterwards, the generals of the warring armies had been immortalized in history books, which feature brave photos of them in uniform, although none of them had ever set foot on the battlefield itself. The truth was, no meaningful measure of land or anything else was gained by either side during the six months of fighting. However, many things had been lost.

Sophie was seventeen years old when the soldiers first came. The French soldiers in their red pants came first, followed by the Brits and the Irish. They engaged the Germans and Austrians in a catastrophic struggle. Soon, there were thousands, and then hundreds of thousands of soldiers, fighting nearly every day back and forth across the river Somme. As the battles raged, the fields of grain and rye quickly became massive graveyards. There were guns and artillery, and the killings began in mass on July 1, 1916, and did not end until the winter freeze. The shells from both sides destroyed every home, business, barn and outhouse in Sophie's village and killed her parents and almost everyone else she had ever known. Historians would write later that the villagers were 'collateral damage' because the barrels of the big guns melted a little under the constant hot barrages and then did not shoot straight, so the shells veered off and struck the village instead of the enemy. Nearly all the villagers died, although it was accidental. Sophie, like an angel or a ghost, remained, and braver than any soldier, moved from house to house, and ruin to ruin, administering to the damaged bodies and souls of her neighbors. Some died while holding her hand. Some lived, and for the rest of their lives, thanked the angel and ghost who had saved them.

One day a young British soldier lay wounded in a pasture where Sophie was moving quickly to help a neighbor whose house was burning. She heard the soldier groan and saw him move. She used the English she had learned in school.

"Stay there!" she called out. "I will be back."

At the far farmhouse, she found the farmer dead and his wife moaning on the ground, with a foot-long splinter from an exploded fence protruding from her throat. The woman's eyes were wild with fear and pain, but she calmed when Sophie took her hand. Then the woman's eyes seem to fix on something that might have happened long ago, and she slipped away into that memory. Her eyes closed, she sighed, and her breathing stopped. Sophie wept, said a prayer, kissed the woman's hand and laid it on her breast. Then the dirt around her seemed to turn inside out, and a huge roar mixed with the dirt and concussions from consecutive bombs, exploding in the field outside, knocked her to the ground. The farmhouse shuddered and collapsed behind her and a heavy crossbeam slammed into the ground near her head. She jumped up quickly and ran down the pathway away from the bombs. She saw the soldier trying to stand up, using his rifle for leverage.

"More shells are coming," he said.

"I know where to go!"

Sophie ran to him, wrapped her arm around his waist and pulled his arm over her shoulder. He groaned in pain, but she pulled him forward.

"Come on. We have to move!" she said. "It's not far!"

He did the best he could, but she mostly carried him to the cellar of her neighbor's farmhouse. She held him with one hand and threw the cellar door open with the other. They stumbled inside and half-fell to the floor. The shells began exploding. The noise was deafening, Boom! Boom! Boom! Boom! and the dirt walls shook violently. Dozens of explosions pounded the earth. It seemed to Sophie as though the shells were going off inside her head. She screamed. He reached for her and they held each other. The shelling went on for more than an hour. It was almost nightfall before the concussive shaking, shattering noises and terror stopped.

They lay together then, exhausted. She pulled one of her arms away and in the darkness, smelled blood.

"You are hurt."

He moaned.

She had helped her neighbor store canned fruit in that cellar and she quickly found a lamp and lit it.

"Where?"

"In the shoulder and in the knee, too, I'm afraid," he said. "There is a first-aid kit in my pack."

She unbuttoned his tunic and then his shirt. A bullet had torn through his bicep muscle. It had exited cleanly, but the wound was still bleeding. She found gauze and a cloth wrap. A small bottle of iodine was in the kit and she carefully wiped away the blood, put iodine on the wound and then stopped the bleeding with the dressing. He groaned loudly but did not flinch.

She then turned to his knee. His blood-soaked pants were ripped from ankle to hip, and an artillery shell fragment the size of her hand stuck out of his thigh, just above the knee. She readied a long gauze strip and soaked a bandage in the iodine.

"Ready?" she asked.

He nodded.

She gripped the black fragment and pulled. It came out past the pink muscle and white bone, followed by a pulsing bubbling of blood. She pushed the muscle back and quickly applied the bandage. She wrapped the gauze tightly around his leg and tied it off.

He lay breathing hard for a long moment and then sat up and grasped her hand.

"Thank you."

She nodded and squeezed his hand.

In the lamp light, she could see that he was only a little older than she was. He was handsome, but she recognized the distant stare of a battlefield soldier in his eyes. He had already been in war for more than a year and he had seen death and had caused death. His dark hair was short. He was not tall, but he was lean, and his eyes softened as he looked at her. She had seen the look before. She knew he was a soldier who just wanted to come home for a moment and be safe. She put her arm around him, and he folded under.

There was morphine in the kit, and she made him take some. He held her hand as he fell asleep.

In the early hours of the morning, before the sun and the bombardment arrived, he stirred, and she could feel his hands move to her hair and then her shoulder and arms. She lay still, and he murmured and kissed her gently on her neck. She turned onto her side and kissed him, and they lay together like that for a long time, murmuring, holding and letting the warmth of each other's bodies try to block out the war. Then, slowly, she unbuttoned his shirt and then her own. His hands went to her warm breasts, and he moaned. Soon all their clothes were gone, and they moved against each other under the blanket in the silence and the dark.

Afterward, when they were resting in each other's arms, the bombardment began. It lasted three days.

There was canned food in the cellar, and they lit candles and went outside only to relieve themselves and only then when the bombardment waned for a moment. They held each other at night, and sometimes during the days when the bombing was especially bad, he cried.

"My friends die every day out there," he said. He tried, but could not stand, let alone walk or fight.

She usually let him cry silently by himself as she found things to do in the cellar. The explosions continued to loosen pieces of earth from the ceiling, and they fell around them and on them, but the walls held. She took the big pieces and threw them out the cellar door.

She kept clean dressings on his wounds, which stopped bleeding and there was no infection.

On the second day, they asked questions about each other. She liked the dark-haired Englishman. He told her his father was Irish, but he lived in London and his mother was Jewish. Her family had lived in Germany before moving to England. His father owned and ran a small restaurant, and his mother handled the paperwork, bills, and family. He told her he wanted to become an engineer and build bridges, not blow them up. He was tender and loved to watch her move about. She allowed herself the fanciful feeling that if somehow they could stay together in that cellar, the war would end, the village would come back to life and there would be flowers again along the walkway. At night, he held her tightly and she slept easily and deeply and wondered if love was something like that.

It was after the explosions stopped that he left. They hugged and cried for a long time. They walked together up the stairs and out the door that led out of the cellar and the sun was bright. He turned and kissed her one last time. Then he adjusted his backpack, strapped his rifle over his shoulder and marched down the road. He looked back once, his eyes full of tears. She knew then she wouldn't see him again. The war was too big. Less than two months later she learned he had been killed when a German shell fell directly into a bomb crater, he and two other soldiers had dived into, hoping to find shelter.

She survived dully during the days after he left and before the war ended. She thought about nothing but searched every day for survivors in the smoking ruins of the village. She found a few and saved some of them. The bombing stopped because the war had moved up the Somme River Valley. She slept in a half-burned barn because the cellar was too full of memories.

When the British, French and American troops won back the small piece of land where the village had stood, they marched back on the roads and gave her food. They warned her the Germans were threatening and could overrun the area. She knew she had to leave. There was nothing left anyway. No buildings or houses stood anymore. There were smoking rafters, broken black chimneys, and splintered fences and barns everywhere. The former little green town was now a scorched, burned sore on the earth.

She was given rides on French army trucks to a train station a few miles away. She slept one night under the trees by the river where she saw the body of a soldier float by. She couldn't drink the water after that. After two days, she reached a small railway station where trains carried wounded soldiers back to Paris.

She talked to a French sergeant, who agreed to let her on the train as long as she acted as a nurse for the soldiers. She told him she would have done that anyway.

Chapter 4

Robert Meeshon was fifty-three years old, but he was more than six feet tall and still fit. He had a broad, trusting smile and thick hair that was bushy and black, mixed with the advancing gray. He had served in the Army as a young man and had been at San Juan Hill with Teddy Roosevelt. An enemy bullet had grazed the side of his face, and he bore a slight scar the rest of his life. It gave him a rakish look that he didn't mind, but he laughed about it whenever anyone brought it up. He didn't mind war stories, as long as they weren't his own.

After the Army, he had been hired at Scribner and Sons in New York, where he'd worked with Margaret's father for several years. He'd taken the position of chief editor that opened in Scribner's Paris office, and quickly become part of the artists' community, providing equal parts encouragement, advice and small loans.

When we got there, he wore a loose shirt and jacket, and held a glass of beer with one large hand. His other hand lay lightly over the hand of his wife, Allison, who was his age and beautiful. She had long brown hair and was casually, but elegantly dressed. Her hands were long and graceful, and her cheekbones were Nordic and finely etched. She had an air of patience and softness about her.

I'd never before seen a couple more comfortable with each other. I was to learn that wherever I was with them, I felt I was home.

Robert crushed Margaret in a bear hug. She squealed a little and hugged him back. Allison watched them for a moment, and then turned to me and extended her hand.

"You must be Jake. So very nice to meet you, I'm Allison."

"Jake! You look like a newspaperman!" Robert roared, turning to clap me heartily on the back. Margaret still held him around his stomach. "Welcome to Paris!"

I shook Allison's hand and couldn't help but study her face for a moment. It was extraordinary; fine, strong, and perfectly set with blue eyes so clear it was hard to turn away. Robert laughed. He had seen the effect his wife had on men many times before.

"Well done, Jake, you can now describe her in your first book!" Robert said, smiling broadly. "Allison is worth many books!"

I grinned, feeling a little exposed and self-conscious, but those kinds of feelings always disappeared fast when I was around the Meeshons. Margaret ordered a crème café and I ordered a beer.

"I say, you have a hell of an assignment," Robert said.

"Yes," I said.

"He's nervous," Margaret said, with a bit of the devil.

"That's good!" said Robert. "You should always be nervous when you're doing something right."

Allison smiled.

"Can I ask you a question?" I said.

Robert pulled back in mock surprise and laughed. "A journalist asking if he can ask a question? What is this?"

Allison and Margaret laughed too. I didn't mind.

"Why didn't you take this assignment?"

"He knows them too well," Allison said. "And they all owe him money."

"It's true," Robert said, smiling broadly. "I do know them too well and they do owe me money. If I told what I know, it wouldn't be a true story."

I looked at Robert and he looked back. I came slowly to understand what he meant. He saw the understanding arrive in my eyes and he was both pleased and amused.

"You will get this in a way I cannot," he said. "Just don't do it before you do it. That's how journalists get it wrong. They work out how the story should be in their heads before they meet their subjects. When they do that, they always get it wrong."

"He thinks they are gods," said Margaret. More devilry.

Robert was amused. "Gods indeed. Maybe they are, and maybe they aren't. That's the fun of it, isn't it?"

He then surprised me by turning to Margaret. "What do you think?"

"I think some of them are gods," she said, looking away, out the window and down the street.

"Ah, and you, Jake?"

I was embarrassed.

"No."

"Ah," Robert Meeshon said again, and he laughed a small laugh. I thought he could see right through my lie.

In truth, they scared me to death. They were some of the best writers and artists in the world. To hell with them! But they still scared me to death.

For the rest of the morning and into the afternoon, he talked about the people I was to interview and made suggestions for angles, questions and even places to hold the interviews. We talked about *them*: Hemingway, Fitzgerald, Picasso, Pound, Stein, Faulkner, Passos, and the others.

We talked about them, just like that.

The bellman was lounging against the door when we got back, smoking a big thick cigar. He had set a glass of wine on the ledge that rose up to a green hedge with blue flowers that surrounded the walkway into the hotel. His bellman's suit was a size too small, but he had one button of his coat buttoned anyway. It looked as if it might burst open. It made me want to keep an eye on it.

"Hello back again," he said, in his working English.

Margaret was high on the wine, the night air, and Paris.

"*Bonsoir,*" she said, giving him an exaggerated curtsy. He smiled broadly, his cigar clenched between his teeth. I noticed that it wasn't lit, but he didn't seem to care.

"*Je suis enchante',*" he said to Margaret.

"Easy buster," I said with a hint of menace, even though I had no idea what he'd said. He didn't know what I'd said either, but in the manner of men, we understood each other. For a second, we stood squaring off, glaring.

He took the unlit cigar slowly out of his mouth and said in a voice filled with wonder, "Well then." He said it in casual, perfect English. I didn't expect that and before I knew it, I started to laugh. Margaret laughed too. The bellman looked at us and knew instinctively, in the strange way most men knew, that the moment to fight had passed forever and from that point onward we would be comrades, sharing secrets if they came up, and sacred bonds. Margaret seemed to know it, too, and she made a sweet, triumphant noise and kissed the bellman on the cheek.

"*Merci! Merci!*" he cried, and he opened the door for his two drunk guests with a bow and a big sweep of his arms. We laughed and stumbled our way back to our room. With the door still open, I took her in my arms and dipped her slowly toward the floor. She flung her arms out in a dramatic dancer's move, her long golden hair falling as she arched her back and neck. Insane for her, I leaned down and kissed her firm breasts and nipples through the thin silk of her gown. She moaned perfectly and seductively, and after that, I made love to her until deep into the Paris night.

Chapter 5

That night I dreamed of a black dog and then of my mother and father. My mother was sitting in our living room in the old farmhouse and in my dream, she was the way she had been during my childhood. Like many Scandinavian women, she was quiet, smart and independent. She lived much of her life inside the books she and my dad borrowed every month from the Kansas City Library, the most magnificent building I had ever seen when I was a boy. I was awed by it – gods lived there I decided one day.

I was outside trying to spy on a pair of field rabbits among the rows of corn. The big summer cumulus clouds were rising, and the heat shimmered off the flat fields. It seemed to me I could see the gothic façade of the library hovering inside the clouds that rose up like mystical legends over our farm.

My mother and father loved each other, in their way, but most often, their lives moved through the skies apart as each dreamed different dreams of Valhalla. Each was separate, but somehow equally insulated from the harsh realities of the Kansas winters, and the periodic droughts when the crops turned crisp and worthless in the fields.

I spent the summers of my youth in those fields with my father, trying to be perfect like him and like the gods in those clouds. I only saw my father cry one time. It was in the afternoon on a bad day in December, when my mother died quietly of influenza. My father followed her by dying six months later. The doctors never determined the exact cause.

I was awake by the time the sun climbed above the curtains and spilled into our room. I swung out of bed and walked softly to the window. Outside, the street was once again moving and alive. The red and blue berries were there, and women in hats sifted through the green vegetables and strung-up meats. I did not see the big American. Two trucks blocked the narrow roadway as workmen hurriedly pulled crates of lettuce, tomatoes and ripe melons off the flatbeds and put them in the stalls. A taxi waited impatiently on the street behind the trucks. I could smell the bread again, but that morning I was distracted. I put my hands on the windowsill and was surprised to find they were full of moisture. Sweat. I was nervous. Who wouldn't have been? I was going to meet the first of *them* that day.

"Jake, how is it?" To my surprise, Margaret was already awake.

"The street?"

"Paris, silly," she said. "And you."

"Okay, we're both okay, I think."

She laughed. "It's going to be all right. You are good you know."

"Thank you."

"You can get better, though."

"Thank you."

"Don't be sore."

For the first time, I was sore. Her words felt harsh, and the worst part of it was that from some rugged, backroom, scarred part of me, I heard whispers that they were true. I wasn't perfect, and I needed to be. I wondered, with some fear, what they would think of me. What did gods think of mortals? I felt ashamed. A black hole was opening inside my stomach, chest and heart that had no dimensions, and I feared I might disappear into it. I covered as best as I could.

"It's a fine day," I said. "The people across the street have opened their windows."

"Hmm," she said. She knew what I was feeling, or at least suspected.

"We're going to meet at La Closerie des Lilas," I said.

"Of course, it is one of their favorites. Are you ready?"

"Yes."

"You should be ready, you know."

I tried to ignore that. To hell with that. I knew I was, at least, ready. As I always did before serious interviews, which meant the ones I really cared about, I already had developed the questions. I had learned that approach from an English professor, tough old Joe Bell at Kansas University. "Make up fifty questions on the big ones and don't be afraid to free-lance off those," Joe Bell had told us in his rough, gravelly voice. It was as good a piece of advice as I ever had received in school. Most instructors didn't know anything about writing, really. They went on and on and looked altogether heroic while giving their critiques of the masters, but in truth, they didn't know much about the real thing, like fishermen who had never caught a fish. That day, I was going to bring my fifty questions – and my ability to free-lance off them – to some of those who lived in the big summer cumulus clouds that rose whenever the heat shimmered up from the hard-baked earth. The Sentinels.

A man shouted something in French from the street, and although I didn't know what he said, it sounded like music. The sound got me caught up in Paris again, and I got fierce inside. It didn't matter what they would think of me or my questions. I didn't care. I told myself that somehow, my life was going to change because of this. How could it not? How many times did one get to walk in Olympus? They were silly thoughts, maybe, but they were mine, at that time.

Chapter 6

I looked at Margaret. She had raised herself up to talk to me, but now she sighed and slid back under the covers. Her blonde hair spilled out onto the pillows. The side of her face slid down in perfect harmony to a perfect nose and then her mouth, which was a sharp slice of strawberries, above her up-tilted chin. She seemed to be sleeping, but she didn't seem relaxed, any more than a cat seemed relaxed when it slept. There was always a waiting action there, a curled, coiled type of tension that made you want to walk with care around it, but there was also something intensely beautiful and dangerous about it. The cat caught the mesmerized mouse. Was I the mouse? I laughed for a moment, but deeper down, I didn't like the idea or the metaphor. No man wanted to be a mouse, and I frowned, realizing I was battling my own thoughts. I decided I'd better do something, so I began gathering my pens and notebooks and placing them in my relaxed old leather briefcase. I tried to let it all go, but I knew I was spinning, as I usually did before big interviews. It wasn't a bad sign. I let my imagination and brain run down a green hill, through the woods, across the river and back, and sometimes straight up into the air like a burst of streaking light just before I went in, just as an athlete shook his body out before a run.

It was the way I relaxed, but always, just for a moment, I would suffer a blinding fear that someday I wouldn't be able to stop the spinning and would walk into an interview and make no sense whatsoever or say something completely ridiculous. It hadn't ever happened that way, but I always suffered from that moment of doubt.

I watched Margaret in the bed for a moment. Then I finished packing and slipped out the door for coffee.

Downstairs, people were moving with purpose. Maids were knocking on doors, businessmen were bustling in and out of the lobby, and a bellman, I hadn't seen before nodded as I stepped out of the lift.

"*Bonjour,*" he said.

I said it back, passed through the lobby and went outside. The air was cold. It felt perfect. I breathed in as much as I could as I walked down the street. I was lost in thought, when a woman, walking as quickly as I was, came around the corner and barged into me. The collision knocked her sideways and she skidded a little, like a small ship glancing off a landing dock. Before she toppled over, I grabbed her around the waist and brought her back up.

She let out a small cry.

"I am sorry!" I cried. "I was walking too fast."

She wriggled to get free.

"Are you all right?" I asked.

She backed away a step and brushed her coat. "*Oui,* but you were walking too fast!" she said curtly, in a heavy accent. "Why do you walk so fast?"

I couldn't help but smile. It was such a French question. Nobody in America would have wondered why anyone else was walking fast. Fast was the speed of America in 1925. In

France, one had to have a specific reason to walk fast.

"I am an American," I said.

"Of course," she said. "You Americans are all gangsters. Only gangsters who do not know anything at all walk so fast."

I laughed. She was angry, but it wasn't all anger.

She looked at me fully. She had an immediately captivating look, Gallic lines and strong, finely thrust chin. Her hair was shiny black under a green scarf; her eyes green and brown, still held a bit of anger, but were not afraid.

"And, so, what would an American gangster be doing in Paris? I thought you were all in Chicago and New York, trying to sell your booze." There was a hint of tease.

"No, we are all in Paris now. We are looking for art and culture and maybe for a ministry. We want to convert."

She looked at me, laughed for a moment and then frowned. "Ha! No, I think you are already an artist, or you want to be. You'll need to be cleverer, though, and more insightful. You need to walk more slowly and see life around you."

What she'd said staggered me a little, as something that you know is true often did, not matter how it was delivered, but I tried to hide it. "Ahh, but then I would not have met you. But you are right, we are all gangsters and we do walk too fast and we are always sorry later."

"No," she said simply. "That will not do. You must apologize more fully right now and then you can go."

I was tempted to continue the repartee' by telling her gangsters didn't apologize but I thought better of it.

"Of course," I said, bowing slightly. *"Je suis vraiment desole."*

She pulled one side of her mouth down and made a

dubious face. *"Mon dieu.* Your accent is terrible," she said, shaking her head. She then looked at me for a long moment, with deep interest. It was a look I would see one more time in the future, but under far more unlikely circumstances. She reached down and held my hand for a moment. It was not a sexual move or even a sign of affection, it was something more, as if she could see into the future. Then she brushed past me. She walked a few steps, turned, stared at me once more and said, *"Au-revoir,"* and then she walked on.

I watched her go and then ducked inside a coffee and pastry shop, ordered a café' and took it outside. The air was still cold. The little cup of black coffee didn't last long, and I was restless anyway. The wind was still blowing when I headed back up the street, and this time it felt rough, but I liked it. My mind wasn't spinning anymore, my collision with the French woman had driven that out of me. I was getting a bit nervous and focused. I found myself wondering what things I would learn that afternoon. What would this great writer say to me? What would he say that would change everything? I knew something would be there. I wondered what my father would have thought about my being in Paris and getting ready to interview one of the gods of my time, and his time.

He would have hoped I would be perfect but expect less. I knew that. Maybe he wouldn't have wanted to hear about it. Maybe he already had imagined the way the gods were, and any other information would have been disappointing and therefore discarded. Maybe he would have been angry about the trespass. I couldn't land on any solid conclusion because I did not totally know my father's head and certainly not his heart.

For a moment, though, I told myself to think he would have been happy and excited about what I was doing. I stayed on that thought for as long as I could before it fell away.

When it went away, a bad feeling came in to take its place, and I didn't like it. I went into a street *marche'* and bought two round loaves of hard bread and slices of cheese. I tried out my faltering French on the shop keeper, who laughed good-naturedly with his mouth open and then bid me *"Au-revoir."* The sun came out, and the bad feeling faded as I walked to the hotel.

Margaret was up and by the mirror brushing her hair when I came in. She seemed lost in thought. Then she turned, and putting her brush in her lap, pinned me with a question in a way some women could do.

"Did you like your mother?" she asked.

My instinct was to run, but I realized that unless I perished in some unexpected way, in a typhoon maybe, (not likely in Paris), I was not going to escape. I tried to stall.

"What?"

"Jake, you never talk about her. I want to know if you liked her or was she too honest for you?"

"That's a crack," I said. "Too honest."

"No, I'm serious. Did you like her?"

I instantly weighed, as men do, whether it would be less painful to fight, or to give in. I gave in, as most men do, most of the time. Maybe it won't last long I hoped, as most men do.

"Yes, I liked her."

Margaret stamped her foot. "What do you mean, you liked her? What does that mean? Did you like her because she was your mother or because of how she treated you?"

That was a complicated question and I knew the footing here could be treacherous.

"Both, I guess," I said, trying not to sound as if I were trying to get out of answering.

"What do you mean, both?" she demanded. "I wonder if she liked you, or whether you frustrated her. Did she like you?"

"Sure," I said. For a moment I debated whether to try to joke my way out of it, but that rarely worked with Margaret and usually prolonged her inquisitions. I also knew I needed to add something. If men were sensitive, they knew when to add things and when to cut things short. They can't always know, of course, because most women know what they are doing. Dancing, I'd always felt, is but a physical manifestation of this action, and it benefitted all men to learn a woman's rhythm in conversation and in dance. Of course, nothing was fool proof.

"She thought I was fine."

As in most cases with mothers and sons, that was not always true. When I was young, my shoes were usually full of dirt, my head was often in the clouds and I obeyed most of my father's rules. I knew that sometimes annoyed my mother because although she was not a rule-breaker herself, I realized later that she had wanted me to be free so she wouldn't feel so alone.

"I don't think she thought you were fine," Margaret frowned. "I don't think she may have liked you all that much. But, that's okay, you turned out okay."

The bad feeling came back, and I turned away and took the loaves out of the bag. I broke off a piece and put a slice of cheese on it.

"My mother would have loved it here, I'm sorry she never got to see Paris," I said.

Margaret didn't respond, but she seemed satisfied now and began to hum as she started again to brush her hair.

Chapter 7

Later in the morning we walked up the boulevards and crossed the Luxembourg Gardens. There were no boats on the lake yet, and it was as still as a mirror, waiting for the afternoon winds to ruffle it up and drive the small waves up and lapping the shore. A few old men were bowling on the lawn under the trees. We saw the clock high on the Palace, and it was a pleasant walk down Boulevard Saint-Michel to the Closerie des Lilas.

Robert and Allison Meeshon were sitting at an outside table and they waved to us. It made me feel good to see them. Robert gave Margaret a crushing hug. Allison kissed me on both cheeks, and then leaned back and gave me a look. It was quick, like a burst of music when a door opened and in an instant, it was gone. However, like a skilled surgeon, she had implanted something inside me, and then sewn me up, as good as new, but with something inside. In her eyes had been a question: *"What are you doing?"* It was a damn good question, I thought, and it took my breath away for a moment, but then Robert grabbed me by the shoulder, and shook my hand, smiling and warm.

"Good to see you, Jake," he said. "You're going to have quite a day."

"Yes," I said. "Thank you for saying that. It assumes I won't make a mess of it."

Margaret frowned.

Allison laughed. "Who cares if you do, Jake? Everyone makes a mess of things and nobody cares in Paris. With him, you'll probably only get one question in anyway. He'll do the talking."

"You should be prepared, though," said Robert. "He will know if you are not and he won't like it, and your interview might not go well."

"I am," I said. And I was. That part of the game I had mastered. Robert ordered cafés for us all. We had a little time before the interview was to start. The writer was coming to meet us. For some reason, that bothered me a little. I had always envisioned that I should go meet them, not the other way around. I thought they were superior to me. I had never questioned that concept, but later I realized that sometimes things we've held sacred for a long time make little sense once we dig them up and hold them up to the light of day. Perhaps, then, it would be good for us, one by one, to dig up all the things we believe in and hold sacred and hold them up to the light of day to make certain they are what we think they are. Not all of them at once, of course, because that causes too much chaos, and we might turn back. But, all of them, sooner or later. I was thinking about all of that when I felt Robert, Allison and Margaret staring at me.

Robert laughed. "Where did you go? We thought we lost you."

"How good is he?" I asked.

Robert didn't answer right away.

"Tell him," said Allison.

"The best," said Robert. "There is no one near him, when he writes his best."

Margaret shook her head smartly. "I don't think so," she said. "He writes too much about fishing and bullfighting and that's boring except some of the things about bullfighters are interesting."

"He does love to talk about those things, but the way he does it is always like a good story and he's interesting," said Allison.

Margaret looked at Robert and then at me. She put her chin out. "If he talks too much, ask him what he knows about love," she said. "That should shut him up. It always shuts men up."

I blew out a breath.

Allison laughed, and Robert shook his head. "Sure, Jake but make certain you have the interview done by then."

I tried to relax. I took a deep breath. I was going to meet *him*, one of *them*, and they were perfect. I had met them before, of course, in the cumulous vapors high above the waving grain fields when I worried about getting the rows perfectly straight for my father. I met them at the great library and whenever my father talked about how I should have been, and how I rarely was. I had longed to someday meet the impossibly perfect gods, but I didn't know really what they looked like. I only knew they were greater than I was, and the only way one could not fall into the black hole of failure, where there was an unimaginable bottom, was to be as perfect as they were, even if there was little chance of success.

A little wind picked its way up the street and the umbrellas outside tilted from one side to the other like awkward dancers. A Frenchman on a bicycle came up the street into the wind, winding his way between the people and the taxis. The bicyclist wore a suit and sat on the saddle in proper style, as though he was in church. Robert and Allison watched him ride by and drank their cafés. Margaret had gotten up and was looking at the French gowns displayed in the dress shop window next door. She really concentrated when she was looking at clothes, like a general studying battle plans.

I knew we still had almost a half hour, so I sipped the coffee and sat quietly for a moment. The street slowly filled up. People moved up and down the boulevard. Many stopped in at the café'.

"We should eat a bite before he comes," said Robert.

I nodded. Interviewing during lunch never worked for me because I would be hungry. I couldn't eat anything when asking questions and writing down answers. You never went into an interview when you were hungry or impatient. Mostly, people liked to talk about themselves and if you wanted to be a decent journalist, you needed to be able to listen, even if you disliked them. Especially if you disliked them. I hadn't disliked many people I'd interviewed. Sometimes, though, I had to sit there and listen to some man or woman who felt they owned the world and me. I could hear it in the words they said, but mostly I could see they didn't smile all the way down when they smiled, there always seemed to be something hidden underneath. Like a snake or a spider. I got so I could tell.

We ordered some sandwiches, ham and cheese on baguettes. Margaret waved to us from across the street but kept up her perambulations. Her arms were crossed, and her focus was fierce.

The steaming cup felt good in my hands because the air was still cool. Allison shivered a little against the wind and without any extra motion, Robert placed his coat around her shoulders. She kissed him quickly on the neck as he leaned over her. I loved them. The scent of warm croissants rode out the door of the café and across our table on the little wind. The sun spilled over the top of the buildings and lit everything like a stage.

"Paris seems perfect to me," I said when the sandwiches came. "What is it like living here? What do you become?"

It sounded like a silly question, after I asked it, but I didn't care. For one thing, Margaret was out of earshot.

Allison cocked her head and looked at Robert.

"Perfect?" he said, looking at me with a slight smile. "I suppose it is in some ways. But how can something be perfect, if it is perfect only in some ways, but not always and not in all ways? But that doesn't make it not perfect does it?"

We were all quiet, thinking about that for a moment, and then we laughed.

"Bravo!" Allison cried.

"Maybe that's the real definition of Paris, though," Robert said. "As far as what you become, I don't know, Jake. But Paris will have something to say about it. If you are lucky and maybe if you aren't afraid of it, it will be a part of you for the rest of your life no matter where you are. It's the finest place in the world, if you aren't afraid."

Then Margaret came back.

"I didn't see a thing," she said. "I thought I might. What are you all talking about?"

Robert and I were trying to figure out how to answer when we saw a large man dressed in an inexpensive, but nicely fitting black suit and white shirt, striding purposefully toward us. He had long, thick legs but walked with a slight limp. He was handsome, with a mustache and combed-back hair as black as a crow's wing. He had an air about him, and I wondered what was going to happen.

Chapter 8

He waved to Robert and Allison from the street. As he walked up between the tables toward us, his eyes fixed on Margaret, lingered for a moment, and then slid over to me. They were the strangest eyes I'd ever seen. There was no color in them, they were black, I guess, but they were open wide and out of them shot an intensity that seemed combustible. Unchecked, ungoverned and in the end, ungovernable. For some reason, I pictured, for half a second, a locomotive barreling down the tracks toward a mountain range where the tracks ended and perhaps the locomotive would run without slowing through where the tracks ended and then test itself against the mountain. It seemed the barreling was almost predestined. I was in awe. Only a god would have tested himself against a mountain.

"Allison! My God you are beautiful!" the writer said, causing a few people to turn around at the noise.

She rose and he grabbed her in a bear hug.

"Thank…" was all she could manage before he enveloped her.

He released her quickly though, as men who respected other men did, and he grabbed Robert's hand, pumped it, and slapped him on the back.

"Roberto, damn it, man, you look fit as a bull!" he shouted.

"Thank you, Champ!" Robert said, using the man's nickname, one of them anyway. "A fine suit! It's good to see you. It's good to see you before you get too famous."

The man laughed and slapped Robert on the back again. Then he turned to us and looked at Margaret. The sun caught her blonde hair at that moment, and it exploded all over like a gold strike. "Splendid!" he shouted, and then he grinned and nodded as Robert quickly introduced us. "Hello," he said to me and then he gave Margaret a full-on hug, lifting her onto her toes. She gasped and giggled perfectly, and I wasn't mad because any man – and most women – would have been tempted to hug Margaret when she looked like that.

He turned back to me, instantly professional, although not cold, and shook my hand with decorum. I was, at that moment, close to flying apart. It was *him*, one of *them*.

"How do you do?" I said, and instantly felt silly. *How do you do?*

"Fine, thank you. Thank you," he said, saving me a little by shaking my hand vigorously. "Good to meet you, old boy. Always good to meet a fellow journalist."

A fellow journalist? I was a fellow journalist?

He was the center of attention for the next ten minutes. The conversation ranged from Robert's work and Allison's art, to the health of Margaret's father.

"He thinks you are wonderful," Margaret said. "He says you are the next Turgenev."

That pleased the writer who made no secret of his admiration of Turgenev. He then shared his feelings about his recent trip to Spain with another writer to pick up a car.

"A disaster," the writer said, although I noticed that later he included a few chapters about it in his book about Paris being a moveable feast. He and Robert chatted for a few moments about French politics and then it was time for us to be alone. Robert, Allison and a reluctant Margaret left to take a walk so I could begin the interview.

We maneuvered our chairs to his liking, so he could sit with the ankle of his right leg resting on the knee of his left. That way he could look past me when he wanted, at about a fifteen-degree angle. It gave him the superior position. I was facing him like a schoolboy listening to a lecture. My initial sense was that he was what a god must be and what my father had thought they were. It thrilled me to know that my father had been right, that gods did exist, and that somehow perfection floated above and through the clouds and sometime alighted on the earth.

He sat in his suit, big, smelling like something I did not know – it was not an unpleasant scent, but it wasn't perfumed like a dandy, either. It was more like cognac and leather. I never told anyone of that because another man's scent was usually a taboo thing for another man to talk about, so I didn't. But it was there, and it was part of his closeness. He filled up all the space around us, and his presence was monstrous, as a father's is to a boy when the boy has done something wrong that requires the father to sit close and explain something important about life.

The secret is boys rarely listen to those lectures because the father is too big and too close and shuts everything else down.

The writer looked up to make sure Robert and Allison were out of hearing.

Then he said, "What makes you think you can interview me?"

At that moment, the planets nudged slightly out of alignment.

I had no answer. With all my questions, I had no answers.

"I don't know," I stuttered. "I have good questions."

He scoffed. "What would you know about it? I should interview myself. You are the lowest of all writers. Novelists are at the top, then non-fiction book writers and then, at the bottom are the magazine hacks. Hacking it out, without any structure, without any form, without anything, really. Hack, hack, hack."

That turned out to be one of the highlights of the interview. For the next thirty minutes, I was boxed around the ring, pummeled in the corners, trapped against the ropes, and battered down to the canvas. I tried to stay with my fifty questions, but he ignored them and simply continued the onslaught. I had no defense. My own boxing skills were not even thought of, it was too devastating. I was shell-shocked and unable to think, react or even feel.

Sometimes during the brief half-hour he allotted to me that morning, when he looked at me I felt as though deep down he had started to laugh, as though he were having me on, and although he was rude and rough, I got the particular feeling he was not altogether serious. I didn't know what to make of that. I just observed it for the moment, but I was still scrambling around trying to find what was left of my dignity and my interviewing skills, which seemed to have temporarily disappeared off the table. I did not think he was bent on inflicting pain, although he didn't mind it much either. It was as if he was standing back and enjoying the situation, as though it was just a scene that had some tension and emotion, one he might use later in one of his books.

I forced myself to study my notes.

"How much of your short stories are autobiographic?" I asked.

"Autobiographic? Good God, man, is that a word? Did you learn that in school? You should unlearn it. I won't answer a question with *autobiographic* in it."

I laughed, but it came out more like a choking sound.

"What I meant was, do you use experiences you had as a child in your stories?"

"Sometimes," he said, looking at me as though I were a new species of beetle. "All writers do this. What else do we know?"

"Right," I said, furiously writing, "What else do we know?" in my notes.

"Are there writers that you admire or who inspire you?" I asked, using question number six on my list. I was a little comforted that I still had a sheetful left.

"Sure," he said, with a small smirk on his handsome face. "Every bad writer who ever lived, and that is almost all of them. Whenever I read bad writing it inspires me never to leave more horror in the world than there already is. Every person has a book inside them and for almost all of them, that's where it should stay."

He smiled a little when he said that, and he seemed larger than ever. His scent was powerful, though not in a way that made me want to retreat. It was more like the heavy fragrance from an endless wall of heroic books in a burnished wood library that would have been hard, and intimidating had it not been altered by the touch of a woman, who let shafts of light in and kept it from being stiflingly male. I got the impression the writer had such a woman in his life, who let the light in and kept him from being stiflingly male. *Stiflingly?* I was glad I hadn't said that word out loud. I had no idea what I was talking or thinking about. I sat silently for a moment, staring and trying to gather my wits. He squinted at me, leaned back, and took a healthy draft from his glass of beer.

"Nothing is the way you think it is going to be," he said. "That is what you need to know, whether you stay in Paris or not and whether you decide you really want to be a writer or not. If you don't know that, either you will become deathly dull, or the world will kill you. Either way you will be dead."

All I could do was nod sagely as though that meant something deeply important to me. At the time, I had no idea what he was saying. My brain had taken a walk without me somewhere down rue Mouffetard.

"Are you working on a book right now?"

"No, I am talking to you."

"Oh. What about later on today?"

He actually laughed at that. "A writer writes whenever he can."

"Yes," I said, and I immediately flinched inside, knowing I had just made it sound as though we were writing brethren, who automatically knew such things.

"Is your next book on war?"

"On war?" he said, frowning. "No one writes 'on war' unless they are historians, and then I would not say they are writers but chroniclers, mere stenographers of the past. Are you planning to write on war?"

"I meant, does your book have a war backdrop and setting?"

"Who said I have a next book?"

"You said a writer always writes, when he can."

"Yes, and sometimes he just has a good beer interrupted."

He speared me with a look from his intense black eyes.

"Let me ask you," he said. "What difference does it make if it has a 'war backdrop' or is about love, hate, honor, betrayal, cowardice or some other thing? What is the difference?"

I felt the cliff face fall away and suddenly I was plunging.

"People will want to know."

"People do not care. They care that you make it seem like what is happening is happening to them. They want to be there and feel it. Then, after they close the book, it doesn't have to be real, because they can take the emotion away with them. It is the feeling that is real to them, and that is why they don't care about the other part."

He took one more long drink of his beer and looked out across the tables, which were now filled with Parisians and Americans, Brits and some others. It was a fine, bright day, but I did not feel it. Two beautiful women had moved in and were being seated, with some fanfare by the waiters, at a table directly in the writer's sight. He was looking at them, and not at me when he said, "Do not ask me how many words I write every day, or when I write or what my inspiration is. If you ask me those things, I will either walk away or, better yet, punch you in the nose."

He was smiling, but just for a moment, an old stirring, maybe born in the hard winds on our farm in Kansas, blew up and I wondered which one of us would punch the other in the nose.

"No, I wasn't going to ask you those things," I said, mentally crossing off numbers twenty and twenty-one off my list. "Are you going to return to New York any time soon?"

"Hmm, perhaps," he said, frowning again. "Is that the best you can do? I think we're done, then."

He stood, shoving his glass of beer into middle of the table. He looked briefly at me, and then turned and walked away. I put my pencil down and stared at his broad back. He stopped briefly to talk to the two beautiful women at their table and then without looking back, crossed the street, turned a corner and was gone.

Just like that.

For a moment, after he disappeared, I felt as though everyone turned to stare at me, with contempt or pity – take your pick – but in truth, no one was looking at all. It was Paris in the bright afternoon. Life went on. It didn't feel that way to me. I felt as though I first had to pull an icepick out of my chest. My notes were scribbles and half-finished words, and I knew I was in trouble because I couldn't remember a word he'd said. All I could remember right then were his eyes and the smirk on his face that made me think he wasn't altogether serious about his insults toward me. Still, I was devastated. Outwardly, I tried to stay calm while I drank the rest of my beer, but inside I was in a free-fall. The cliff was crumbling, and I was falling with it and on top of it all was my father's profile and the overwhelming sense that I had failed.

Chapter 9

The train to Paris took three days because so many soldiers were headed north, and it took a long time to board the wounded. Sophie worked constantly. She did what she could, changing dressings and bandages and throwing the blood-soaked old ones off the train. There was no other place to put them and discarding them kept the disease down.

On the afternoon of the first day on the train, she was surprised to see a childhood friend, Cassandra, whom she had known in school.

They hurried toward each other between the seats full of wounded men.

"Sophie!" Cassie shouted. She threw her arms around her friend.

"Cassie! It can't be you!"

Cassie began to cry. She sobbed and could not speak.

Sophie hugged her and felt the girl shaking.

"Come," she said. "There is an empty bench. Let's sit."

On the bench, Cassie finally stopped crying.

She told Sophie, in a flat soft voice that everything in

her village had been blown apart and then burned. Each army had marched through the village several times and each had blown something up until there was nothing left.

Sophie saw how frail she was. Cassie's eyes, which were surrounded by her unkempt auburn hair, worried Sophie. They were haunted, frightened and deeply angry.

"I hate soldiers," Cassie said as the train stopped to take on more wounded. "I don't understand any of it. Why do soldiers want so badly to kill each other? They all die so easily. And they kill and kill and kill. They killed my parents, my auntie and uncle, my cousins and my friends and where my house was -- there is nothing left. Nothing. There isn't even enough of it left to burn."

Cassie was lost, and she seemed to sink deep into her seat.

Sophie leaned over and put her arms around the girl. Cassie's skin felt cold.

"We mustn't think of it," Sophie said. "Not now, not yet. I don't know about wars, except I know I hate them."

Cassie stopped crying after a while, but she seemed to continue to shrink as though trying to disappear. She was taller than Sophie, but somehow seemed no bigger than a child.

"Cassie, are you hungry? You must eat something."

The frail girl shook her head, but Sophie pulled an apple and a piece of bread from her small suitcase.

Cassie would not eat them.

"Paris will be okay," Sophie said. "We can find a safe place there. We will be safe from soldiers and everything else. Maybe we can even go to the ballet."

"Yes," Cassie said slowly. "I remember when we danced

in the gardens when the roses were out."

"Me, too!" Sophie cried. "The roses were beautiful. There are roses all over Paris. Cassie, we must always be friends now. You were a wonderful friend. We'll find more gardens and we'll dance again."

Cassie smiled a little but did not say anything more for a while. She looked out the window for a long time, watching the green French countryside. Then, without looking back from the window, she whispered,

"Where was God, Sophie? Where was God?"

Sophie tried to find an answer, but none came immediately to her. Cassie sighed and then leaned her head against Sophie's shoulder and fell fast asleep.

On the second day on the train, a young Canadian soldier began to hemorrhage. He had a chest wound that erupted blood onto his comrades and it poured down the aisle. Sophie and Cassie were summoned by a frantic sergeant. They raced through the cars until they reached the stricken soldier. He lay alone on a bench, gasping and crying out. The other soldiers had backed away. Sophie reached him first. Cassie saw him and, horrified, tried to stop. She slipped on the blood and fell, sliding a few feet on the slippery surface. She screamed and began crawling, covered in blood. She crawled past Sophie to the door of the next car and disappeared.

Sophie took gauze from her kit and pushed it against the spout of blood. It shot out in all directions, but she covered it with her hands and pressed down until she stopped it. Then she quickly wrapped strips of cloth around his chest. The bleeding stopped. The soldier looked at her. His breathing was labored. She wiped the blood off his face and leaned down.

"You are going to be all right," she said. "It's okay, now. It's okay."

He looked up at her and tried to speak but couldn't.

"Shh," she said. "Your parents are here, and so is your sweetheart."

He lay back and closed his eyes.

She looked around to the other soldiers. She pointed at one, who did not seem badly injured.

"You! Watch him. When the bandages are soaked, come get me. I'll put on new ones. Do it!"

The soldier's face was ashen, but he nodded.

Sophie left and hurried up the aisle to the next car and the next.

Cassie was nowhere in sight.

She hurried up through several cars. Finally, she saw Cassie standing outside on a small iron platform. Sophie pulled open the sliding door to the outside.

"Cassie! What are you doing? Are you okay?"

Cassie was startled. She backed up against the railing, staring at Sophie with wild eyes. She looked like a ghost. She hooked her heel into one of the lower railings and lifted herself up. Sophie realized she was about to jump backward off the train.

"No!" she shouted. She grabbed Cassie by the arm and pulled her back.

"What are you doing? You don't want to do that! Come with me. Come back in!"

Cassie let Sophie pull her away from the railing. She didn't say anything. She didn't cry, she just stood on the platform, motionless and mute.

"Come on. We can't be out here."

The girl let Sophie lead her back in and down the car to a bathroom. Sophie cleaned them up as best as she could. She kept her arm around Cassie, and they walked back to their seats.

"It's not much longer," Sophie whispered. "The world will change. You'll see. The sun is coming out. No more soldiers. I need you. We'll find the roses together. You'll see."

Cassie said nothing. The train raced on toward Paris.

Chapter 10

Once they reached the city, Cassie was met by her grandparents, who took her into their home to the north. Sophie found a small apartment by herself near the hospital, where she had found work within a week of arriving in Paris. Over time, Sophie saw less and less of Cassie. When they did manage to get together, Cassie seemed increasingly withdrawn. Sophie suggested Cassie check into the hospital, but Cassie refused, and Sophie did not see her again for months.

At the hospital, Sophie settled in quickly, working long days. She rarely took time off to see the city or do much other than sleep. She did not want time to think. At night, she shut out thoughts of her family from her mind, but she did allow memories of the Englishman in, sometimes. She tried not to think of him with sadness but focused only on the three days and nights they'd spent away and safe, how he'd looked at her and how they had tried to stop time. She didn't try to define what had happened but knew that it didn't seem wrong. In fact, it seemed beautiful and sad at the same time. The memory was powerful. It remained so strong that sometimes she thought she could feel it in her fingers. She thought of the white dove she'd seen one day and thought its wings might feel something like that. She saved the feeling inside.

There were other men interested in Sophie. Doctors, patients, the butcher on the corner, and most of the young men, and older men, she passed on the street inhaled quickly and watched her go by. She could have had an encounter with any of them, but inside she was still not ready.

She had, though, taken up painting again. Her mother had always loved art and there always had been brushes, easels, oils and canvases around in her well-lit art room. Sophie had sat and watched her mother paint until the time she was given a brush herself.

Her mother had been inspired by the ambitious and rebellious life and art of Suzanne Valadon and told Sophie stories about her when they painted together. Valadon had grown up in poverty, worked in a factory making funeral wreaths, and then a market selling vegetables and finally joined the circus. Sophie was fascinated. She'd been amazed when her mother told her Valadon fell off the trapeze and had to go into another line of work, modeling for artists in Paris. Her mother had seemed to drift into a different world when she told Sophie of how artists such as Renoir, Degas and Henri de Toulouse-Lautrec had fallen in love with Suzanne and painted her.

Sophie had been enchanted the entire time she spent in her mother's art room. Women were not encouraged to become artists in those days, but her mother hadn't cared. The rebellious, self-confident and passionate figure of Suzanne Valadon had inspired them, and Sophie's father had done nothing to stand in their way. He would walk in occasionally, slowly, with a soft smile on his face, aware that the room was a female inner-sanctum and he was but a lucky guest. He always had complimented their paintings, careful to pick out the best qualities.

Once in Paris, Sophie set up an easel by the window in her front room and tried to recreate the feeling she'd had with her mother. Usually it was good, but sometimes the good feeling went away when something reminded her too sharply of her childhood. Sometimes a brush stroke would bring back memories, and she would leave the apartment and take a walk.

She worked at the hospital most days and some nights. She learned the technical parts of nursing quickly and efficiently, and that was where her only problems arose. She had seen many different kinds of wounds during the war, when she was often left by herself to bandage and fix the wounded. She often saw the doctors at the hospital, who had seen no action, make poor decisions with the patients. She spoke up at first, but the doctors severely reprimanded her.

"You are a nurse," they would say. "Not a doctor."

She argued with them in the first few weeks, but then realized she would lose her position if she kept confronting them. After that, she kept quiet, mostly, but after the doctors left the rooms, she treated the patients the way she knew was right. Since they often recovered with astonishing quickness, the doctors learned to leave her alone and then take credit for the healing. It annoyed her, but she had other things on her mind.

Chapter 11

I had to escape the café. I threw everything into my satchel and hurriedly walked out to the street. I had no idea where to go, but I knew I couldn't go back to the hotel or anywhere where I would know anyone.

"How did it go?" they would ask.

So, I walked quickly, as though the world might think I was a man of great purpose, perhaps an international business tycoon or art dealer, or maybe I was going to meet a lover – no, not that. That would have been a different walk altogether. I turned right onto rue du Cardinal and right again onto Boulevard Saint-Germain, with all its rattling traffic, and made my way across the flat Pont-de-Sully Bridge and down Quai Henri IV on the other side.

My satchel of half-completed notes was over my shoulder and flapping lightly on my back hip. A stream of French children, innocent and awkward in their shorts and buttoned-down shirts, came pouring like a spring torrent toward me, jumping, skipping and flinging their book bags around in the air. It must have been the beginning of a holiday from school and their joy was fresh, but I didn't care. I couldn't shake being enshrouded in his big black coat and his big black eyes that judged me impersonally before he stood and abruptly walked away. The noisy children split around me and skipped on.

I crossed the river again at Pont d'Austerlitz and walked back up the Quai Saint-Bernard to where the artists were lined up along the West Bank, all of them concentrating on adding a touch here or there on their canvases or putting a touch here or there on the rich tourists walking by. On most days, the artists would have drawn me, but this time, I ignored them and walked down the slopes to the river. The current was still in shadow and there were dark swirls and dangerous eddies which suited my mood. A hatless man without any shoelaces in his tattered shoes sat down at the edge of the water, drinking red wine from a bottle without a label. I saw no boats out, just heavy water swirling silently past, like the huge, endless back of a dragon, quiet and crouching, moving down there well below where the people were. Up above, it was noisy, especially where the children were. But down here, the dragon moved quietly, without notice, except for those who felt drawn to it, who needed its hidden power and promise of a dark and quick death. It was a melodramatic and melancholy river right then.

I sat some distance from the man with the wine bottle and watched the swirls and eddies. Although those who have seen the likes of the Nile, Congo, Mississippi, and the mighty Amazon, might have considered the flow of the Seine effete, they would have changed their minds quickly if they found themselves caught in the river's strong, dark undercurrents.

I watched until the boats started to come by again, barges mostly, but a white yacht came by too, to sample the Expo and the Paris life for a while. None of it brightened my mood. There was nothing to be done about that. I didn't know what I had expected from the interview, but it wasn't to walk away feeling like I had been pummeled in a prize fight. The man below me on the bank took a long drink from the bottle and then put it down in the grass and his head slowly sank down onto his chest. There was some grass on the bank and black starlings flew by. Swallows, which lived under the bridges, flew faster around them. I suffered without connecting the suffering to reason, and that meant I just keep suffering with no real method of stopping it except waiting for time to take the edge off. Time, that day, went by slowly. The sun just sat in the sky, not moving, not blinking and not shedding its warmth.

Finally, my melancholy met the one thing it could never overcome, hunger. It wasn't the first time a quick upswing of hunger pangs had saved me from a lost or sad mood. The scent of something fine in the restaurant ovens above came stealing down from the street above, and I forgot all about being sad and walked quickly up the quay and then down past the artists to the boulangerie, where new bread the color of gold was just being placed in the front window. I bought a sandwich, bit into it, and immediately felt better. I walked a little, back toward the river, sat on the rock wall that kept civilization from crumbling into the primitive ever-moving current, and ate the sandwich. I saw the man with the wine still sitting on the riverbank. I went back, bought a fresh loaf and gave it to him. He took it and said nothing.

A short time later, I remembered I had agreed to meet with Robert later that afternoon to let him know how things had gone. I wasn't looking forward to the meeting and the thought brought me down again. I knew that no matter what I said, he would know it had flopped, and that I had not handled the interview well. I didn't like the thought of Robert Meeshon looking at me the way my father used to look at me. The image of their faces comingled in my mind, and it made me mad. It was a quick anger that came up before I knew and recognized it, and I suddenly and wildly punched the nearest thing to me that was not human, a sign in front of a coffee joint that boasted, in French, "The finest café in Paris." The sign snapped off and clattered along the ground, startling a dozen patrons outside at the tables, most of whom had cups of the finest café in Paris in their hands. A woman stifled a scream, and two men rose from their chairs. They glared at me with stern French faces, but I could tell, with some small satisfaction, that they had no desire to venture any closer to me. I was a mad American for the moment, and I just stared back at them, not really seeing anyone, lost in my head. Without thinking, I shrugged, picked up the sign, hung it back up and walked on. The two men sat back down, the women went back to their cups, and the soft pattering French conversations took up again.

Chapter 12

"**A**h, he was like that," Robert said, even before I said anything. I had walked through that part of Paris, past where they wrote, painted, and as I was to learn later, drank, made love to people other than their partners, and lived lives of debauchery and melodrama I had never dreamed existed. I met Robert at the Café du Dome. He was sitting when I came in. He didn't get up but motioned to the chair across the small table. I sat, but I had no answer.

"I was afraid he might do that," Robert said, pursing his lips and shaking his head. "Did he give you anything?"

"Not much," I said.

Robert looked at me, cocking his head slightly. He stared at me openly for a long moment, and when he spoke, his welcoming attitude had changed slightly.

"Is that right?"

"I don't know. He didn't say much. Then he just left."

"It isn't going to be the same in Paris," Robert said.

I had no idea what that meant.

Robert continued, with some obvious effort. "It isn't always the language that matters here, Jake, it is what comes in-between the words sometimes."

Frustrated, I sighed and shoved my beer into the middle of the table. I realized I was doing exactly what the writer had done just before he got up and left the interview.

"I don't know what that means," I said, letting more irritation show than I wanted.

Robert simply nodded his shaggy head, smiled a little and reached over and patted me on the arm in a way that was okay with men. It was okay with me, but I still didn't know what he'd meant, and I was still sinking; the small hole below the water line was getting bigger.

"It's hard to explain, Jake. I don't think I can explain it. But maybe he gave you all you needed, and maybe he gave you all there is. Maybe you don't see it yet."

I felt despair creeping around the corner. I should have known what Robert was saying, but it sounded like gibberish. That's all there was? What was all there was? That was outrageous, and I did not believe it. I believed the writer had cheated me, even though he knew the rules of the game. I was annoyed, and the conversation was not helping. Robert saw that, checked his watch and stood up. "I am sorry, Jake. It will work out. I have to go. Don't forget tomorrow morning and your interview with the painter, and then the party later this week. Allison is expecting you."

I nodded, somewhat sorry I had offended him, but not sorry to see him go. I needed some time to get past my anger. After he left, I thought about the interview I had the next morning with one of the world's greatest painters, at least according to people who knew more about art than I did. I wasn't sure, but I knew he usually went by only one name.

The thought of walking back to the hotel to develop another fifty questions for him was too much. I paid the check and went out onto the street. The cold wind slipped inside my shirt and pushed up my neck. The Cathedral of Notre Dame was suddenly there in front of me and it looked to me as if one of the gargoyles, with his pointed chin cupped in his hands, shook his reptilian-like head at me. I shook my fist back at him, made a rude gesture and then walked faster into the wind, along the thick and ancient rock wall that separated the street from the dark river below.

***

Underneath, under a shelf of earth and rock, supported by heavy timbers built by the city's engineers years ago, a black dog played for a while along the bank. Its tail was high as it happily chased the small ground squirrels into their dens, catching none of them, but zigging and zagging through the dusty, barren edges. Sometimes the dog dramatically jumped and snapped at a starling or two, but the birds banked out of harm's way and zoomed past him with ease. The dog finally turned and trotted back under the shelf and eased through a door-sized opening in the back. It slowed to a walk and followed a tunnel that was tall and wide enough to allow three men to walk upright, side-by-side. The tunnel traveled into the hillside for about fifty feet, and then led to a heavy wooden door, braced in three places with thick, dark iron. The dog scratched at the bottom of the door. In a few moments, the door opened, and a short, dark-haired man leaned down and scratched the dog behind both ears. The dog's tongue hung out happily and its tail beat back and forth rapidly in the air.

"Boy!" the man said, stroking the dog.

The man and the dog turned and walked down steps to a huge room that opened up on all sides. Large doors at the outside of the roughly circular chamber led off in many directions. A number of people were in the room, some sleeping in the far, dark corners and some cooking over an open flame that released a beckoning scent of fresh peppers, lamb and seasonings.

Two women were tending the large cook-fire, and there were other women, men, and children moving about. The children were playing a game and laughing, kicking a tight ball made of red yarn. One of the men was patching a line of shoes, and two others carefully picked through several wallets in a pile near the fire. Two were removing the paper bills and counting them into envelopes. They selected out all the other contents, too, keeping what could be sold or bartered and throwing the rest into the fire.

In a crib nearby, a baby was fussing. Two older women came over and took turns tending to the young mother and the baby, saying soothing words, bringing new, warm towels and sheets, and washing the baby with clean cloths. They hugged the mother and patted her knees. She smiled at them and the baby quieted and soon fell asleep. The mother slept too, and the women moved silently around her, one slipping a pillow under her head, and another floating a slight blanket around her. The small man with the dark hair walked to the woman who had laid the blanket and put his arms around her. She smiled and kissed him. Her hand dangled down and caressed his thigh. The dog wandered over to the side of the fire where he was out of the way of the women and contentedly flopped down onto the warm floor.

Chapter 13

The year 1925 was the season of the celebration of Art Deco in Paris. I wasn't sure whether I liked Art Deco, but the French did. So did the Italians, or at least some of them did with a true *passion de l'art*, but I was not in the mood for it. It seemed not much more than mural after mural of tall, lithe, and mostly nude courtesans, which under normal circumstances had its allure, but right then, it seemed pretentious and struck no chord in me. Only later, when I came back to it, did I realize it was supposed to be like that. Then it was okay, and even grand, like opera. But right then I had the urge to write "Fraud" across it. However, no such impoliteness could ever have been allowed from a man from the American Midwest. Still, I felt no other stirrings in the murals and felt, with a sneer, that most of the magic and poetry of art deco were in its name. But had I seen the *Mona Lisa* at that moment, I might have said it lacked expression.

I was not looking forward to my looming conversation with Margaret. To tell her the truth, that the writer had given me little and had been arrogant and boorish, and left me without so much as a goodbye, was to hand her an open invitation to humiliation. And it would come. She would consider my performance a colossal failure that reflected badly upon her. Worse, she would somehow, let me know that she could have done better. "He would have liked me," she would say, her eyes flickering like a hummingbird's wing for a moment before coming back to still. The flicker, I knew, would be meant for me to realize he would have found her immensely desirable and wanted her, perhaps right there spread-legged on the table, if he could have had her. Of course, I knew she would be right, and I knew we would both ignore it and not say anything about it, but we both would know it was there.

It was not yet late afternoon and the streets were not crowded as I walked all around the Luxembourg Gardens and down Notre-Dame des Champs, by L'Observatoire, and back out through the gardens to the Quai aux Fleurs. Walking across the bridge toward me, ramrod straight and perhaps belonging in a different time, was a man dressed in a French military uniform. He wore dark red pants, a blue tunic with heavy, tan leather shoulder suspenders and an empty revolver holster on his thick, tan leather belt. An empty scabbard flapped against his leg. The only non-military clothing he wore was a red beret. His pants were tucked into shiny knee-high boots. The first question that ran through my mind was why the French chose red pants when they marched into war. I would not have wanted to give the enemy that kind of target. Then I wondered what he was doing. The uniform was the type the French had worn early in the war. Most men who had worn that uniform had fallen before 1916, and certainly by the end of the summer that year, the rest had been buried under the banks of the Somme. But he was alive, if in some other place.

As I got closer, I saw his eyes were lifted above the skyline and had a distance to them. I had been too young for that war, my father too old, but my father joined anyway, and they had taken him. He'd fought in the American Army for two years all over northern France and he'd come back different. He'd rarely talked about it other than one time, when he had had too many shots of whiskey he made in the cellar. I was fifteen years old, we were outside on the porch, watching the stars. It was quiet until my dad started singing an old army song I'd heard him sing before.

As the moon came up, he started telling me about marching in the mud. At first, it seemed nostalgic and I was relaxed, but then his voice grew serious and angry and he described smelling the chlorine gas and watching Germans die, and watching his friends die, and watching Brits, Italians, Irish and Frenchmen die. Then he'd paused and told me that wars were made by tyrants, kings, presidents and prime ministers.

"They should fight each other," he'd grumbled, the smell of whiskey sour and sweet in the air. "Their fathers, sons, cousins and uncles should all get together and fight each other and whoever wins, wins. Then we should have no more of it. We have it all backward. The farmers, butchers, teachers and students fight and die, but the tyrants and kings don't, yet it is their pictures in the history books, as if they won the war. Most of them never shot a gun or saw a man die. Give them the damn guns if they want a war and let them shoot each other. Let them bleed. Sons o' bitches!" Until I was older, I was always worried and a little ashamed of what he had said.

The ex-soldier in the red pants was now passing me and he looked over and frowned, as if he could tell what I was thinking. How could you tell such a man that all his friends and family were dead because the entire Western

71

World had gone insane? How could you tell him the men who'd fallen, many of whom were his friends, whom he'd watched die in agony and unimaginable pain and fear, had been sucker-punched by arrogant, narcissistic leaders who never had to dodge a bullet themselves? You could not. The heartbreak was too much, so you were mute. You were muzzled, forever. You could not ever say such a thing, but then, because of that, it went on and the living hero went on. He and his red pants crossed the bridge, marching stiffly.

Margaret was sitting in front of the mirror when I got back to the hotel room.

"How was he?" she asked almost breathlessly.

"Fine. He was fine."

"Fine? What does that mean? How did the interview go? Was he fabulous? Did you learn from him? Did he say anything about me?"

"He said to say hello," I said. "We didn't have a chance to chat. It was crowded, and we had to get right into the interview."

She was disappointed, but the hello made her happy for the moment.

"The interview went well. It was short, though. He had another appointment and had to leave quite quickly."

She pouted. "I should have gone." The flicker appeared.

"It wouldn't have mattered," I said roughly.

"I don't think he would have left early, if I'd been there."

"Maybe not."

"Of course not. He would have found something interesting to say. Didn't he say anything interesting?"

"He said it doesn't matter what you write about, although I don't think that's what he actually said."

"What? You aren't making sense. Were you two drinking? Really Jake, the biggest interview of your life and you were drinking? Don't tell anybody. Don't brag about it."

I didn't say anything. It was almost better she thought that. Being a sober failure was too bitter to think about.

Margaret moved away, still shaking her head, but the drinking element seemed to make her feel better.

"You cannot understand these men," she said thoughtfully. "You can get some of what they say and think, but they are different and maybe someday you can understand, but right now, you can't do what they do. You need to keep your wits about you. No more drinking, Jake. Maybe have a sip of beer or something like that, or not even that, but you have to do whatever you can to keep up."

The light filtered through the French lace at the window and projected onto her face the kind of pattern one saw in art, on canvas and I was lost again. I promised her I wouldn't drink anymore.

I took my satchel to the kitchen and laid it on the table. The light came in there too. The table was lit, but it didn't reveal anything more than half-written sentences, words scribbled hurriedly in the margins and, in large letters, "Nothing is the way you think it is going to be." What the hell did that mean? I sat down and sighed, looking over the notes. I kept coming back to that. Was that supposed to be some sort of writerly sophisticate? A magnificent insight hidden in poetry? Or was it just bullshit? Bullshit from a god? Was he killing me? I traced the notes with my fingers, running them over his words, hoping perhaps to feel them in a way I could not understand them, but it didn't work. I went to the cupboard, got myself a piece of cheese and some bread and opened a cold beer from the ice box.

Chapter 14

The second interview did not go significantly better than the first. Robert Meeshon had set it up. It was with a man who was destined to become the most famous artist in the world, and he was already well on his way to becoming that when I met him at a small table in the back of the Dome. The artist was short in stature, but his eyes were huge, expressive and full of energy and it wasn't hard to see he was used to being at the vortex of all social interaction.

My father had lectured long during the quiet of the frozen nights of the Kansas winters about the importance of humility. He had thought it as important as talent, perhaps elemental to the very foundation of a man. The artist did not share such a thought. He was vain and commanding and those he couldn't command he berated or ignored. With almost every look and sentence, he mocked my father's theories. The artist, unlike the writer, did not talk sparingly, but went on with volume, passion and detail about his work, his vision and his 'undeniable leadership' of modern art. He often spoke of himself in the third person and it seemed to me he would have been surprised, in fact he wouldn't have understood, if anyone disagreed with his artistic outlook on the various movements and schisms with which he was busy revolutionizing the entire world of art.

His own paintings, drawings and sculptures were angular and geometric in nature and could almost have been seen and interpreted as easily on their sides and upside down, and he was especially enthusiastic about the techniques he had used in his newest painting of three dancers. He elaborated for some time. I nodded at the appropriate times, but truthfully, I had no idea what he was talking about.

His eyes darted from place to place as he talked, then they would settle on something. As rough as he was, his eyes reminded me of small birds, delicate, soft, and wary of the world.

Suddenly, he looked right at me. "They ought to put the eyes out of painters like they did goldfinches, in order that they might sing better," he said.

I didn't know what to say for a moment.

"I didn't know they put the eyes out of goldfinches," I said, finally.

"They do."

"It sounds barbaric and damn difficult."

"You are being literal. You are a journalist, not a novelist.

"I like goldfinches." I shrugged.

He smiled a little, but the exchange didn't slow him down.

He talked on for several moments and then said, "You deal with truth in your newspapers, or at least you think you do. But artists do not. We all know that art is not truth. Art is a lie that makes us realize the truth. What you do is write the truth to make us realize the lie. At least that is what you try to do. Who knows who succeeds?"

I shrugged. "I do not know."

"I know," he said triumphantly. "I succeed. Give me a museum, and I will fill it."

He smiled, amused at my struggle for a reaction. For the rest of the afternoon, the interview was a run-on, one-sided conversation that peaked and then waned and, in the end, the artist seemed to lose interest entirely. He looked around the bar and promptly announced he was leaving. Many of the patrons at the bar lifted their glasses to him and he smiled sublimely, bowed slightly and walked out. He made no indication that he even remembered I was there.

For the second time in as many days, I struck out and walked the streets of Paris alone, not wanting to talk to Robert, Margaret or anybody else. Things felt strange after that. It was as though I had never walked or seen those streets before or the sidewalks, the women picking fruit out of the barrels, the men smoking and walking about in their endlessly moving line of fedoras, or the way the vendors shouted out instructions as they moved in more barrels of fat apples and ripe peaches for the women to pick through.

It wasn't just the city that felt strange. I felt as though everything inside were strange, too. Insecurity could be a mean thing and it swallowed me up on the streets of Paris as did a terrible feeling that I was sinking. There wasn't anything I could do but jam my hands into my coat pockets and start walking fast. I tried to breathe and focus on my breathing, but doubt had gotten into my gut. The interview and the one before had tilted everything I knew on its head. These successful, godlike artists were so arrogant and dismissive, and I was so incredibly naïve. It was then the entire foundation of my life started to shake. My father told me repeatedly, as I was growing up, that "Only great men do great things." He wanted so badly to believe in perfection. It was like a religion. He believed life wasn't about striving to be perfect, it was about being perfect. Growing up in a small town surrounded by vast acres of corn and wheat fields, I had extremely limited access to outside information. His vision had been the major tenet of my understanding of life. Now I had no idea what any of it meant.

I walked for hours, not knowing or caring exactly where I was. I crossed the heavy bridges and saw the swift water that carried the barges and small boats below. I walked, numb and silent. The sun was at a low slant and again the wind picked up and brought a chill. I leaned into it and that brought me back to the street. I realized I had no idea where I was.

I began looking for a street sign when I saw a woman coming out of an apothecary shop across the street, carrying in both hands bags of medical supplies. She was young and pretty and appeared strong, but there was something else about her that captured my attention. She had the indefinable presence that some women have and that nearly every man recognizes and wants, even for a moment. There was something almost mystically elevating about such women. This is not meant physically, although that may come later, but rather it's a healthy mix of emotions that, for men, can even touch the deep and neglected part of hope in their lives. Most men do not give themselves permission to be happy very often, and that kind of woman makes men, who were still open to it, immensely happy for those precious seconds. Joy surges in and for that moment, life hits a pinnacle. After that, often comes a deep appreciation. Most men feel an immediate urge to communicate this to the woman by thanking her or complimenting her, but few women know what the man is really saying or why, and either move on or smile and give a quick 'thank you' for the compliment. This does not instantly change the mood for the man, but it is the beginning of the end to the feeling, although he remains forever grateful for that moment and will often try to recreate it in his mind. Some try to express it through art, although the artist most often knows that only *she* has the ability to fully express this immeasurable gift, but it is in the imperfection of the artist's attempt that acceptance grows, and love becomes possible. It is hard to say if men ever give that kind of gift to women, but for men, it is the treasure above all other treasures. Women give it so easily and freely, without guile and without expectations. It made me think about angels.

I could not help crossing the street toward her. She was struggling with the heavy bags and I hurried to catch up to her. As I did, I hesitated. What the hell was I doing? What was I going to say to her? Would she be frightened and turn hard? I wasn't as afraid of her as I was of losing the feeling from the gift she had just given me. I stepped off to the side so I wouldn't come up close, and I passed her and then, when I was a safe distance ahead, I turned slightly and said with colossal clumsiness, "Those look heavy, can I be of service?" I said it in French. Immediately I wanted to kick myself. *Can I be of service?* What was I thinking?

She smiled though. "No, thank you. I can manage. Are you lost?" she added with a short laugh. I knew my accent was a bad one and she was commenting as much on that as the fact that I truly had no idea where I was.

"*Je suis désolé,*" I said. "*Je ne parle pas bien le français. Mon accent est terrible.*"

"No, no, not so bad," she said in English and she laughed again.

Later, I would wonder where she learned to speak 'American' English, but right then I laughed with her and told her I was indeed lost.

She looked right into my eyes, which was not what I was expecting, and said, "Monsieur, I have a feeling you will find that which you seek."

The formality of her speech was curious. *That which I seek?* Was that a mistake in language on her part or something else? She had captivating eyes.

"Thank you," I said. "I assume you are talking about my hotel?"

She didn't respond other than to give me a small smile.

"To tell the truth, I'm not sure I want to find it right away, anyway. I've been walking around all afternoon avoiding it." I said.

"Some days are good for that," she said. "Sometimes it is better to find a *boulevard enchanté* and let it take you where you need to go."

Who was she?

I glanced down at her bags, which were full of medical supplies.

"Are you a nurse?" I asked.

"Yes." She didn't say more, and we stood there silently for a moment. I wasn't uncomfortable; it was a good feeling. Then she lightly touched my arm and smiled again.

"*Au revoir, mon ami,*" she said.

I liked the sound of that and was thinking hard about an appropriate reply in French, when suddenly, she was gone. I heard her laugh and she walked away, her blue skirt moving in a lovely rhythm. She crossed the street, turned, waved and then disappeared down a boulevard. I stood and looked to the curve of the street where she had disappeared to keep the feeling lingering as long as I could.

The doorman was at the hotel when I got back. He looked at me strangely and was about to say something, when three talkative Italians came through the door and asked him to help them with their luggage. He shrugged and assumed a bored look, as if he were being asked to do a most unpleasant favor. He looked at me and jerked his head a little at them, as if to pull me in on a conspiracy against the presumptuous Italians. Then he looked down away from me and frowned. I sensed something was up, but he was off with the bags before we could talk.

I checked my messages at the desk. I had two: one was from Margaret, saying she had gone out with friends, and one from my editors at *Scribners's Magazine*. They wanted to know how the interviews were going. The question sent a shiver of dread through me. What did I have after two interviews? I had come to interview some of the best artists in the world and I couldn't seem to find the men who matched up to them. How was I supposed to write that? No one, from my editors to my father and especially the readers, would want to hear that. Nor would they believe it. The world needed heroes after the war and what I saw, if it went reported that way, would proclaim them something else entirely. It wasn't the way it was supposed to happen. I knew instinctively that rather than finding revelation in my observations, my readers, editors and Father would find all the fault in me – and I would be fired and forgotten.

I climbed the stairs slowly and went into our room. Margaret's nightgown was draped over the back of the vanity chair. The vanity itself was covered with her things and there were shoes and clothes across the floor and the bed. The clothes were all the latest, beautiful and tailored to perfection. I was certain she didn't ever leave the room without looking sensational. The thought depressed me even more. I took the telegram and my notes out onto the balcony.

There wasn't much in my notes. A few quotes, mostly cut off in the middle, and a few ideas I had jotted down. "Gods of ego," I had written off to the side. I scratched that out. Sometimes editors wanted a guy's notes, and I didn't want them seeing that. I drew other words over it, and then scratched it out again. After the sun dropped lower behind the angled buildings on the other side I felt no better. I went to the wine cabinet and poured myself a Chianti, but it was too sweet, and I poured it out. Restless and growing increasingly anxious, I paced around for a little while, and then grabbed my coat and went back downstairs. The doorman was nowhere in sight. I set off down the street and found a small café with a decent bar. I ordered a whiskey neat and took a mouthful. I welcomed the burning sensation as it went down. I sighed and looked around for the first time. The bar was crowded with men in dark suits and hats. The women wore flowered spring dresses below the knee, silk hosiery and small element shoes. Unlike the loud American bar conversations I was used to, the French and Europeans spoke in a measured volume, with a rhythm and tone that was more like music than conversation. Then I suddenly saw him outside at one of the little tables. The writer sat with his head down, working. I had heard he wrote mostly in the morning, but he was there in the late evening and I watched him carefully. He never looked up or around and did not make any movement that would give him away. He was like a lion deep in the brush and the rest of us were noisy intruders, threatening his habitat, his way of life.

I knew he once had written the following about working out in the public:

"*The blue-backed notebooks, the two pencils and the pencil sharpener (a pocket knife was too wasteful), the marble-topped tables, the smell of early morning, sweeping out and mopping, and luck were all you needed...Some days it went so well that you could make the country so that you could walk into it through the timber to come out into the clearing and work up onto the high ground and see the hills beyond the arm of the lake. A pencil-lead might break off in the conical nose of the pencil sharpener and you would use the small blade of the pen knife to clear it...and then you could slip your arm through the sea-salted leather of your pack strap to lift the pack again, get the other arm through and feel the weight settle on your back and feel the pine needles under your moccasins as you started down for the lake. Then you would hear someone say: 'Hi Hem. What are trying to do? Write in a café?' Your luck had run out and you shut the notebook. It is the worst thing that could happen.*"

I laughed out loud while thinking of those lines. It was curious to look at him working outside at the table with so much going on around him. He actually appeared vulnerable, as if, at any moment, his luck would run out. He wrote with a pencil; he had several lined up to one side of the table. He would write for a time, maybe a paragraph, and then he would pause, sit up straighter and look at what he had just done. Sometimes he would cock his big head, with all the black hair hanging down in front, and begin again, shifting slightly in his chair to give his body a new feel. Then he would be lost to all those around him, and if anyone tried to talk to him, then, he would be slow to respond and when he finally focused on them, it would be with a frown. Then he would give them the kind of hard face that could win an argument without saying a word. I saw him do it to a woman, who slunk away, making her eyes big and giving a mock frightened look to her friends, who laughed at her quick exit from the writer's table. She was an attractive woman, too. It didn't matter when he was writing. That part of him, my father would have appreciated.

I borrowed a napkin and a pen from the bartender and jotted down what I had just seen. It contained more truth than anything I had so far, and I liked it. Gods could be covetous of their work time. That observation, I thought, would be allowed by both editors and readers.

I ordered another whiskey, with ice this time. The sun went down and singing began at the far end of the bar. Most around me joined it, and a few couples got up in a small, open area and began to dance. The song was a new one, *Sweet Georgia Brown.* I hadn't heard it before, but I liked the fast-clipped rhythm and the way the women and men whirled, their feet went heel-to-toe and then ankled outward and they bent their elbows like mock scarecrows. It was all fun and noise and the music was good. Everybody got up and danced, the bar swayed, the music got louder, and the drinks flowed. It was getting rowdier by the moment, when I felt a hand grip my shoulder.

"Do you find Paris amusing?" the writer asked.

I had no idea what to say, but three rounds of whiskey had made me, if not happy or positive, at least willing to say something ridiculous. "This part of it anyway!" I had to shout.

"Ah, but not the other parts?"

"Not so far."

He ordered a whiskey and soda.

"Have you written anything?" he asked.

I wasn't sure exactly what he meant. Had I written anything on the article or anything in my life worth reading?

I looked at him. He smiled, but it wasn't a kind smile. Still, even in his malice, the big man had a sly charm. He had laid a trap and we both knew it. He was enjoying it.

"It's coming along fine," I said, although it wasn't coming along at all.

"Sure, sure it is," he said, and he downed half his whiskey. "My advice kid, is if it is too tough, just give up." Then he laughed loudly for a moment, looked out over the room, got up and walked out the door. Although he didn't look back, he waved over his shoulder as he left.

Chapter 15

Margaret did not come home that night. She left word with the front desk clerk that she and a girlfriend had traveled to Bourges to see her girlfriend's father, who had suddenly taken ill. I didn't like that much. It was not like Margaret not to meticulously plan out every move well in advance and in the morning. But there wasn't much I could do about it. I took off my clothes and went to bed.

In the early silver of dawn, I sat down at the kitchen table, spreading all my notes out across the table. I had a toasted baguette with strawberry jam and a cup of black coffee. I sharpened several pencils and took out my notebook. I looked over my jagged notes and with no one around to distract me, I went right to work. I was supposed to file one article per week, for three consecutive weeks. I hadn't written anything, and I had two days left to file the first one. I took my favorite pencil and wrote:

It is not on Mount Olympus where they gather any more, but on the Left Bank of Paris, where it is no longer possible to walk a mile without bumping into giants of literature, art and music.

I read what I had written, crumpled up the paper, and tossed it away.

Paris, not Rome, London or New York, nor Hong Kong or
Tokyo, is the home of the new Renaissance. No city roars in this,
the Roaring Twenties, quite like it.

I laughed and then groaned at that one. I not only
crumpled the paper, I also shredded it so no one could ever
see those lines. I knew I was trying to write what I thought
everyone else wanted, and I knew that was no good, but
I felt trapped. Nothing felt good or right. I started pacing
around the room. I ate another baguette with jam. That was
when I started feeling my father in the room, and Margaret's
father in the room and Margaret not in the room. She still
hadn't wired as to when she would be back.

I suddenly felt crowded in the room, so I grabbed my
coat and trotted down the stairs and into the street. The
day was overcast and cool. People seemed to be subdued,
walking without smiles and their eyes stayed under their
hats. I felt alone and almost as suffocated as I had in the
room. I walked down rue Mouffetard, but this time even the
market seemed relatively deserted, with only a few reluctant
shoppers taking care of their business as if they wanted to
be somewhere else. I stopped by a bar I didn't know, and it
was almost empty. I ordered a beer. The bartender poured
it without the customary smile, and I drank half of it and
shoved off, feeling even more miserable than ever.

The sidewalk was spotted with raindrops when I went
outside. It was quiet other than the light rain and then I
heard a man start to sing some part of *La Fida Ninfa*. He had
a good voice. His Italian baritone rumbled down the street
and rattled around off the buildings. I couldn't see him, but
the song was full of drama and lament. Listening to it in
the morning amid a lowering mist left me with a peculiar
feeling. There was nothing for it except to let it all in and
work its way through because I knew if I tried to stop certain

feelings, no matter how undefined, they would gain strength somehow. I just tried to breathe and not think.

The raindrops began to combine and come down in bigger drops as I walked. The artists along the bank scurried to cover their canvases, and I decided to go see Robert to talk about the article. I could still hear the baritone for the first few blocks, but when I turned the corner onto Boulevard Saint Germain-des-Pres, the traffic noise drowned him out. I walked fast. It wasn't raining so hard as to make it a bad walk, but I still wanted to be there as quickly as possible. Robert came to the door when I knocked and invited me in. He was with a man, who I thought at first was in a military uniform, but then I realized he was a policeman.

"May I present Monsieur Jean-Claude Gervais, who is an *Inspecteur de Police*, as well as being my long and great friend," said Robert. Both men grinned, their friendship obvious.

"Nice to meet you," the policeman said in perfect English. He had curly black hair streaked with gray. He was tall and angular, with a dark, Algerian face. "I worked with Americans, including my friend Robert here, during the war," he said, seeing the surprise on my face. "They taught me how to speak English like a swell." We laughed, and Robert poured us a glass of wine each.

"Jean-Claude and I met even before the war," Robert said. "We were both students at the Sorbonne. He was studying to be an engineer, and me a journalist. We had lunch at the same time and ate at the same bistro every day. With all the politics in Europe at that time, it wasn't hard to find something to talk about. We've been talking ever since. It's been a good, long time."

The Inspector nodded and grinned. "A long time, yes,

but with a long time left to go!" he said, raising his glass and we all toasted to 'long times'. Then Robert turned to me.

"Apparently, there are some thieves about, and Jean-Claude came by to tell me they are particularly preying on foreigners," he said. "It is a courtesy for him to do this because although I don't think you and I are in any mortal danger, there are others around us whom he thinks we might want to warn. It seems these particular criminals are some of the best pickpockets in Europe. Some call them gypsies. They settle into an area and stay together and protect each other."

"They are not gypsies," said Jean-Claude, "but they are very close, and they are very good. They can slip their fingers through your pants, and you won't feel a thing." Robert smiled ruefully and raised his eyebrows in agreement.

"A den of honorable thieves, it seems, although I don't think those whose wallets they steal might say that," Jean-Claude said. "They stick together and take care of each other, and they aren't violent as far as we know, but they are still thieves. Now, that's a story, Jake. No one seems to know where they are from or anything else about them."

"A moveable culture," I said.

"Yes, from what we know, they coordinate quite well," said Jean-Claude.

"Let me get this straight," I said. "It's a culture of people living together who take from others to sustain their way of life."

"More or less," said Jean-Claude.

"Then it sounds like almost every nation on earth," I said. "They should have their own flag and sing patriotic songs."

Robert laughed. "Good, Jake! Your skepticism is growing. No self-respecting journalist should be without it."

I bowed sitting down. "Thank you, Robert. It's coming more easily than I thought."

Robert looked at me curiously. I had said it with more intensity than I realized.

"Well, then we must treat them like we do the rogue countries of the world," said Jean-Claude. "Which includes every country, at one time or another, of course. But, Jake, it will not hurt to tell your friends and please, if possible, have nothing to do with these thieves! Hopefully, we can catch them, and they can pick each other's pockets in jail."

Jean-Claude stayed for a while and he and Robert talked about their families, the state of the economy, and even the weather. It was clear they enjoyed each other's company, but at last, the Inspector finished his wine, stood, got his hat, smiled and bid us au revoir.

"It was nice to meet you and I will watch out for the *voleuses* especially," I said.

He laughed, embraced me heartily and kissed me on both cheeks. *"Salud,"* he said, then he hesitated and added, *"Prends soin de toi, mon amie, Jake."* Then he went out the door.

When he was gone, I turned to Robert. "Why did he tell me to take care of myself like that?"

"I don't know. Maybe he senses something is going on with you – like I do. Let's have it. How is the article going?"

I shook my head. "I can't seem to get it down."

"What have you found out so far?"

"So far, things I didn't want to know."

Robert looked at me and didn't say anything.

"It isn't what I thought. It's confusing. They don't give, they take. I think maybe they are bastards."

Robert exhaled in a half-laugh. "Bastards, yes. They can be that, and maybe that's all they really are. But, what did you expect them to give to you?"

"I don't know. More of what they give in their art maybe."

"Ah, and what do they give in their art?"

"I don't know. Illumination. Wisdom maybe. I don't know for sure."

"Hmmm."

"I'm not sure what to do. They were so damn arrogant, and I didn't mind that so much as I did the other."

"Other?"

"Yes, they didn't seem like great men in any way that I know."

"Maybe they aren't."

"But how can you say that? They are some of the best artists in the world. That's why I'm here."

"Are you here to tell the truth about them?"

"I don't know."

"You don't know if you are supposed to tell the truth, or you don't know what the truth is?"

"Yes."

Robert laughed.

"When you figure out the answer to the first question, the second will be easy."

Had I come there looking for answers? Maybe. I feared nobody had the answers. My father didn't. He thought so, and I'd never questioned them until now.

"Only great men do great things," I said, repeating my father's line. Then I felt foolish.

Robert looked at me but didn't respond.

I sighed and stood up. "I have to go."

He nodded, extended his hand and shook mine. I left without another word being spoken. He had told me everything he was going to tell me.

Chapter 16

The rain stopped, but the ozone smell was powerful along the boulevards and across the gardens as I walked back. The poet was gone from the park and so was everyone else; it was deserted except for the ducks making quiet V-shaped wakes across the pond. It was late afternoon, and the sky was a delicate twist of iron-gray and black-streaked clouds. I had Paris to myself right then. The long green of the park still glistened with the rain, and the clouds hung heavily in the back over the rooftops of the buildings and houses. It was beautiful, but I was only vaguely aware because I was engaged in making myself miserable on a perfectly fine afternoon. My shoes felt too tight, the occasional splashing of the ducks in the pond sounded irritatingly loud, and a leaf fluttering and spinning down annoyed me greatly. If I had been a dog, I would have bitten a tourist. The air, though, somehow got past my dour mood. It was moist and thickly scented with trees and hedges and maybe a deeply satisfying perfume from the heavens, and whatever it was snuck past and for a moment, balanced things, but that ended when I entered the hotel and smelled the cleaning bleach on the floors.

The doorman saw me and with a frown, ducked down a hallway. I was too preoccupied to care. I had to get upstairs to see what would come out on the paper, the words and most importantly, the attitude, if I even had one. I laid my paper across the table and brought out three pencils. I had a small sharpener inside my satchel and carefully honed the points of all three. I had until the next morning to file my story, and I knew that finishing it was going to take all of that time because I had no idea what I was going to write.

"*He looked tall, heavy, dark, formidable and somehow threatening when you first saw him, and that's exactly how he turned out to be,*" I wrote.

Uh oh. Too many issues with that. First, I wasn't sure if the editors ever ran anything in the second person. Second, "somewhat threatening" might sink the entire ship. Who was I to say a god was threatening? The editors, who most often aligned themselves – at least in their own minds – with the gods, wouldn't want anyone as lowly as me making those kinds of judgments. It just wasn't done. I wasn't even sure it should be done. What then was my attitude?

Just then, Margaret opened the door and swept into the room. She was wearing a long slim, gray silk dress, with a black velvet scarf that trailed to her knees and a matching black velvet bow tied just below her provocative hips. She also had on flawlessly applied bright red lipstick. Margaret always had more attitude than I did.

"Oh, Jake! I am so glad you are here. I was afraid you were out with one of your new girlfriends or something!"

"What? I'm writing."

"Well, I've been out, and it was a most dreadful evening and day. Paulette has a sick father, you know, and we had to spend the entire evening catering to his every wish, which I don't mind, of course, because Paulette really wanted me there and we needed to be there, but still, it was dreadful and I thought about you, of course. I assume you received my message?"

"I'm sorry her father is sick."

"Oh, don't be silly, Jake. There isn't anything you can do about it, and there isn't any need to be sorry because we don't really know him at all, and he seemed a bit harsh on Paulette anyway, so I was glad to leave today. No need to be sorry, dear."

"Hmm," I said.

"Well, did you enjoy yourself last night? I'm sure you must have visited some of the local color. Did you go out with a prostitute, Jake?"

"What! No. What the hell are you talking about?"

"Nothing, I thought maybe you were feeling cooped up and just had to get out and maybe you wanted some fun."

"Jesus, Margaret, of course I didn't go out with a night woman."

"Night woman. How quaint, Jake."

"What's the matter with you?"

"Nothing." She rushed over and wrapped herself around my shoulders. "Jakey, Jake, my poor Jake."

"Why am I 'poor Jake'?"

"You just are. You are wonderful, beautiful, poor, poor Jake."

"Enough," I said, annoyed. "Did you go out to dinner?"

"Dinner?" she asked, suddenly pulling back from me and moving over to empty out her small overnight bag. "Oh yes, I suppose you could call it that. We had the best *coquilles Saint-Jacques*, a lovely *blanquettte de veau*, and wonderful champagne.

"Champagne? It sounds like a celebration."

"Oh, Jake it's Paris. Every night should be a celebration. It's not my fault it's Paris."

It was a strange conversation and I felt something twist in my stomach. She must have felt it, too, because she turned away from me and bent over to take her things out of her suitcase. Suddenly, bending over like that, she was all angles and curves. I didn't know which was more exciting, the angles or the curves, but I knew she was perfect geometrically. My father had planted wheat in long, curving furrows, unspoiled in their symmetry and, in part, I had grown up wandering inside those furrows. Gazing at her was like that. She was long and elegant and swayed slightly as she moved but there was something else there too. Only later would I realize it was a twisting, knife-edged sense of threat, the same thing I felt in my father's presence, but right then I thought that was what love felt like – that it rightfully came with a sense of pain.

But she was completely gone to me now, humming as she straightened up and hung her clothes. There wasn't anything left to do but try to forget what she had said, and how the knife twisted. The moon finally rose above the low dark clouds. The hum from the street below turned soft and my pencils lay lifeless on the table. Margaret continued to hum as she combed her hair. Late that night, well after Margaret had fallen asleep, I lit a candle and tried to write again, but it was no use.

***

Down below, under one of the thick bridges and out of sight from the street and the watchful eyes of Inspecteur de Police Gervais and his men, the community of *voleuses* went through their nightly rituals. The small, dark man petted the black dog and made sure he had water and plenty of stolen lamb for dinner and that his bed, which was made of old rags and torn blankets, but was thick and fluffy and near the embers of the evening's fire, was made. The little thief, whose name was Emile, was married to a woman named Bridgette, who, as much as anyone in the group living in the airy, open cave underneath the city, seemed to be in charge. Emile and several other men sat contentedly in the outer ring around the fire, drinking beer and the red wine that could be taken quietly and unnoticed from the big trucks that sometimes sat unguarded on rue Mouffetard, by the market. The men were surprisingly well-dressed, in similar checked broadcloth shirts and casual, but well-made sweaters. Their trousers were creased and in the corner of the cave hung a number of stylish double-breasted, gray wool suits. The women, who sat between the men and the children, who were nearest the warmth of the fire, also looked as if they belonged to the upper edge of Parisian society. Most wore crepe silk dresses and either poiret sheen or radio tweed coats. Bridgette, who wore a new, knife-pleated silk wrap coat with a four-button radio tweed coat, moved around the large room with confidence. In the back, the men were dividing up the 'take' of the day. This included several wallets, a case of wine, three large sacks of vegetables, two baskets of fruit and five wraps of fine lamb chops. It would feed them for nearly a week. It had been a good day.

A week before, some of the men had come across an open clothing store, after the bored clerk wandered down the street late in the afternoon for a quick glass of Bordeaux. What could a few minutes hurt? No one had come in the store for an hour anyway. The men from the cave had moved quickly through the racks of beautiful clothes, picking out the sizes and styles they needed. Dresses, coats, boots, suits and underwear were quickly thrown into big sacks and carried out the back door. It was probable the clerk didn't even notice the theft until days later when he and others did inventory. By then, it was too late to determine who had been on duty when the theft occurred, although the clerk quietly suspected it might have been on his watch. It was almost a month before he dared to venture down for another Bordeaux.

Bridgette kissed each man on both cheeks. They smiled. She put her hand on Emile's shoulder and bent down and kissed his ear. He held the side of her face with his hand and smiled contentedly. The children soon went to bed, chattering softly, and the women then gathered their men. They all bid each other *bonne nuit* and some said *Fais de beaux reves* and a good feeling was left lingering near the fireplace, where the dog was already sleeping soundly on its side.

Chapter 17

On the other side of the river, a light still burned on the second floor of the hospital. Above, the doves were already night quiet and still. Inside, Sophie sat with a needle and thread, fixing a torn coat pocket belonging to one of her patients.

Her hands moved effortlessly, and her mind went back to the chance encounter she had had on the street with the American. She thought about how awkward he had seemed at first. She smiled when she thought of him asking if he could "be of service," and how he'd winced after he said it. She found herself attracted to him. He had an atrocious accent, but he seemed genuine and was handsome, and it had been fun. Had she flirted just for a moment? Her hands flew through the fixing and she laughed. Yes, of course, but just for a moment. He had seemed not only awkward but also troubled, but that faded away when she teased him. Their interaction had been more than pleasant. He hadn't asked her where she lived or for her number, but she really hadn't given him the chance. Why? Had she wanted him to ask? Yes, but now it was too late.

For a moment, she looked out the window. The lights of Paris blinked as people went to bed. For the first time in a long time, she thought about the war and the Englishman.

She knew the pathology. The raw emotional wounds of the event healed first, then the secondary echoes gradually faded and then, if one was lucky, the trust of life and love came back, and only then was the healing completed. How many times had she shared that with her patients? Saying it and living it were two different things, though, and she was confused about where she was in the process and secretly doubted sometimes whether it always worked.

She took solace in her half-finished painting, sitting on the easel by the window. She had tried to paint a portrait of her mother first, but it hadn't worked out. She'd decided, instead, on a cityscape of Paris – rooftops rising with hope, a pair of doves visible, fluttering, preparing to land. In the back, though, was a dark, menacing, marching line of blue-black clouds. Were they coming or going? She was still looking at it, trying to figure that out.

Somewhere below her balcony and down the quay by the river, a poet, a vagabond from the north, maybe Denmark, was reciting a small poem. The exact words weren't written down, but the essential message was that the breaking of unblemished childhood trust was often the most psychically violent change in a life. It happened to almost all of us, the poet promised, but it is what happened next that divided us. Bad or no healing left jealousy, doubt, anger, and betrayal seething inside people's souls, where the greatest healing left them open to each other. The poet had no answers, but the ragged people who had gathered to listen seemed to like his simple accent. They stayed together for a while after he finished.

***

One day in January, when it was snowing lightly, Sophie received a note from Cassie, asking if they could meet the following day. It was a Sunday, and Sophie did not work until the evening, so they agreed to meet inside a warm café off Saint Germain. Sophie had mixed feelings about meeting Cassie. She was looking forward to seeing her, but at the same time, Cassie reminded her of the village and her family. Sophie had so far been able to keep those memories at bay. She knew it wasn't fair to burden their relationship with those memories, but Sophie couldn't help it. She took a deep breath, reminded herself that her friend needed her, and walked toward Saint-Germain.

Cassie was sitting inside the café when Sophie arrived. She did not look happy, but she brightened and stood quickly when Sophie came through the door.

"I have missed you so!" Cassie cried, throwing her arms around Sophie.

"Me, too," said Sophie, who hid her shock. Cassie was waif-thin, and her face was gaunt and drawn tight. Her eyes were sunken in even farther.

They grasped each other's hands.

"Tell me what is happening," Sophie said.

Cassie frowned and looked up to the ceiling, trying not to cry.

"Nothing. I am doing fine. My grandparents love me. I am fine."

Sophie was silent for a moment.

"Cassie?"

"No, no, no."

"I'm your friend. I went through it too."

Cassie sat silently for several moments. Tears came to her eyes and Sophie feared she was going to collapse.

"Did you?" Cassie finally said, with surprising fierceness. "I didn't see it and I still don't see it! You are fine. How can you be fine? How?"

"Cassie, I am not fine. Not at all. I still can't think about it. I stay awake many nights just trying not to think about it."

The girl was silent, she seemed to have disappeared.

"Cassie. Talk to me."

"Why?"

"Because it's the only way. We have to talk to each other. There is no one else. What we have to do is find something else to do in our lives. We have to move forward. We have to do things every day so we can fill our minds with other things."

"I can't."

"You can. You have to. It isn't easy. Just small things at first. Just try to do small things but do them all the time. You have me, your family, and the angels, if you choose."

Cassie made a contemptuous sound. "Which side was God on?"

"What?"

"Which side was God on in the war, Sophie? Theirs? Ours? I didn't see much of God when everyone was killed. You saw what I saw. Which side was he on?"

"Cassie, God wasn't on anyone's side. This war was made by men."

"I saw a bloody child's foot still in its shoe. I saw tendons and bone sticking out of it. Did God do that? Did he do that? Did he?"

"No. We did that."

Cassie grew angry. Her mouth drew back in a snarl, and she stabbed the air with her finger.

"Then where was God, Sophie? Watching? Was he just watching? How could he just watch and let that happen? There were bits of children all around my village."

Both women were crying. "Cassie, I don't have those kinds of answers. I don't know."

"Then why are we talking?"

"I love you, I care about you, and that's all we have right now. And that has to be enough, for right now." Sophie moved and hugged Cassie, who stood stone still.

"Cassie, all we have left after that is love. We have to believe in it. There is nothing left."

"Do you believe in it?"

Sophie felt like crumbling. Could she lie to her friend?

"I know I care about you and my patients."

"But that isn't what you are talking about."

"Cassie."

Cassie looked at her. Everything seemed to be gone from her. Her face was impassive and completely white. Her eyes were expressionless. "It's okay. It doesn't matter."

"Cassie, it does matter. Come to the hospital with me. There are people there who can help."

"Have they helped you?"

"In a way, yes."

"No, they cannot help me. When I close my eyes, that's all I ever see. The child's foot in the shoe. My parents dead, my uncle and aunt, dead. Everybody dead. Is that what you see?"

"No, I cannot see it even when I try."

"That would be better."

"Cassie, you must try. Maybe you can move in with me and work at the hospital."

Cassie smiled.

"Will God be there too? Watching?"

"Cassie."

"It's okay. I don't mean bad things with that. I just can't close my eyes anymore."

Just then, Cassie's grandparents came through the door of the café and Cassie saw them. They came over. Cassie grasped Sophie's hands for a moment and then kissed her on the cheek.

"Goodbye, love," was all she said before she left.

Chapter 18

Early in the morning, even before the sun made a silver light, a fisherman fell out of his boat. He had gone out early to try to beat the barges to the river because fishing had been slow lately, and he blamed the barges for making the fishing bad, but he'd gotten there too early and the darkness held on stubbornly. He was moving toward the front of his boat, when he tripped over a snarl of lines on the bottom and fell heavily into the water. The end of his life came simply and quickly. His friends searched for him, but the powerful, deep dark currents didn't let him up until long after his lungs filled with the brown water. His boat had drifted ashore, and his friends and the police feared the worst as they searched for him along the riverbank.

The police came after a while and made noises with their sirens, and I heard the sirens and saw them at the river's edge, but did not know until the following day, when the concierge at the hotel told me about it. "People are not careful enough of the river," he said. "It is beautiful, but one is foolish to trust a river. Even the Seine, which looks like the gentlest of all rivers in Europe, will hold you under and kill you without thinking and without any effort at all."

I went up to the room to write. Margaret was there. She reminded me of the upcoming party and ball sponsored by the Meeshons and the magazine, and then she left to meet some friends. It was time to write. First, I skinned and ate an apple, drank a glass of juice, paced and drummed my pencil against the desk. Then I sharpened and re-sharpened the pencils, fidgeted, stood up to get coffee, sat back down again, and then got up to butter my toast.

At noon, I looked down and was somewhat surprised to see I had written nothing. I had thought of twenty beginnings, some middles and a few endings, but none of it had found the paper. An hour later, at least a dozen perfectly crumpled tablet papers were balled up on the floor against the far wall. My efforts escalated to swearing and threatening the paper, but none of it did any good. I tried to focus again, but I wasn't any closer to resolving the conflict that raged in my head. I had expected to write about these gods as my father's gods, and that would have made all the editors happy, but that wasn't the truth. They were, as I saw them, egotists and bastards. They weren't great men doing great things. Yet I was stopped for another reason. Doubt sat on my chest like a great lion that threatened to devour me if I moved at all. What if I was wrong? What if I had missed something, or everything? Maybe what I saw, my truth, was not the truth at all. Maybe these were great men, and I just couldn't see it. I stood up and took my frustration out on the table, crashing my fist down on it so it wobbled and tipped, sending the pencils flying all over and the empty papers fluttering to the floor. The pencils rolled as if they were on strings into the heat vents. I was so mad I couldn't even laugh. I wanted to punch something else, but there was nothing else around, so I finally gave up on being mad, got down on my hands and knees, and tried to fish my pencils out of the heat vent. They had rolled down so far, though, I couldn't get my hands on them.

I stood up and actually felt a sense of relief. Now I could delay the writing for a few minutes because I had no pencils and had to go buy some at the store on the corner. Leaving the apartment was a joy of sorts. The bellman was downstairs and held the door open for me as I went out. He nodded, but his attempt at a smile looked more like a wince. I was in no mood to bother with it. I walked like a free man down the street to the little store.

"Two pencils," I said, ordering in English. When the clerk pretended not to understand, I sighed and walked to the back and took two pencils out of a tray that held writing supplies. I smacked them down onto the counter and cocked my head at him.

"*Oui,*" he said.

He seemed to understand I wasn't to be trifled with, or maybe, to his credit, he sensed I was miserable and was being sympathetic. Either way, I went out and walked back to the hotel. I took my time, but once I was back in the room, the light was still weak, the papers were still blank, and I was still out of ideas. An hour went by, and I did get something down on paper, but it was a story without merit. I gave them what I thought they wanted, or maybe subconsciously, what I thought my father wanted. Whatever it was, it lacked truth, which was the worst sin a journalist could commit.

Exhausted, I gave up. I was angry and frustrated, and I knew even then that I had been beaten by my own past. I just didn't know what to do about it. There wasn't any breathable air in the apartment anymore, so I took my smudged little story and walked, slower this time, five long blocks to the Western Union and had the clerk send it to my editors. The walk back to the hotel was long and dreary and I felt a bone loneliness under the pale streetlamps.

Chapter 19

Paris, in 1925, had a young heart. As the painter had told me, "It takes a long time to become young." I did not understand that until much later.

The city had come through the war with wounds, but cities healed fast and perhaps the only one in the world that could have rivaled Paris in terms of imagination, swagger and optimism was New York. But while New York was powerful, it was still relatively modest in its lifestyles. Paris was elegant, risqué, and completely alive. The culture in Paris ran centuries deep, and after the Great War, the artists had gathered there. They all had their favorite places in the city, but sooner or later they all met near Montparnasse or the West Bank. In the cafés and night places one could always find painters, poets, conductors, sculptors, politicians, ex-soldiers, thieves, and swindlers crowded in. Often, the biggest challenge in the evenings, when the champagne and whiskey flowed and the music from the jazz trumpets grasped everyone in its rhythm, was to tell them apart.

I wandered the streets once more, stopping by some museums to look at the great art. There I could fantasize once more that perfection did exist, if only within frames and in the imagination of a young boy who'd grown up in a Kansas wheat field and had been nourished by a mother who strived to live, feel and be free and a father who simply wanted to believe in things.

As I walked, my attention was drawn to some action by the river. A crowd of men were pulling the body of the fisherman from the water. His face was pinkish-pale and as inflexible as a statue's. Green algae were strung over much of his body. The fisherman's wife was there. I saw her drop to her knees with her hands clutching her face, sobbing with terrible anguish. I doubted any painting in any museum anywhere in the world could have matched the depth of pain and ageless sorrow I saw on the woman's face. I wondered then if the painter had been right – that the stylization of art was meant to save us from the truth of what was playing out in front of me – the worst of life's pain. Was romance the great anesthetic? I didn't like thinking about that.

They placed the body in the ambulance and drove it away. The woman stayed on the dock, in silent collapse. Her friend stood helplessly nearby. The wind picked up and blew coldly across the river, snapping the woman's skirt and blouse and striking my skin like a string of needles. Overall, it was a morning to forget, though I never did.

***

Margaret was out most of the time during the next two days, visiting friends. She said she was shopping for the party. I went with her, once. I thought I was prepared for such an experience, but I was not. For the entire day, she tried on clothes and she asked me to take notes on the clothes so she could remember them later. In the morning, she tried on brocaded border dresses, with sash finishes in the back and a streamer tie of vari-colored novelty silk ribbon. I kept copious notes. But after a few twirls and an over-the-shoulder frown at the mirror, she dismissed each as being "last year's effort," and disappeared again into the jungle of silks, sashes and sighs. She reappeared in a dark green pleated knife skirt with a blousy top full of patterned rectangles, which was replaced with a crepe de chine over-blouse, which was destroyed by yet another over-the-shoulder scowl.

"Hmm," I would say when asked for my opinion, which was every time. At first, I waxed eloquent with sharp and fitting compliments, but after a few of Margaret's quick and rather pointed rebukes, which reminded me of the news reels of marines practicing with their bayonets on straw dummies as they got ready for the war, I began to better understand my role as a quiet and *totally* agreeable audience member in the fitting area.

"It has a certain flair," I learned to say carefully. "Is it the look you want, though?" One had to learn the rhythms of women and for each woman the rhythm was different. If a man was lucky, he could find a rhythm that was much like his own, and the music was sweet and passionate and stayed that way for a long time. If he was unlucky or did not pay attention to the right things, he would never match his lover's rhythm and they would be doomed to a life of stepping on each other's toes.

The play between us continued into the late morning and ended abruptly, when, after much fuss and falderal she settled on a purple, silk wraparound with a plunging neckline that accented her perfect figure such that it nearly took my breath away. It was accented with a sheer, light, golden-yellow silk shawl, and a matching flappers' headband with a delicate, vertical purple blossom tucked behind the left ear. The shawl was filmy and magical and fell from her flawless shoulders to the ground.

"*Très belle Mademoiselle,*" the male clerk said, obviously impressed.

Margaret accepted the compliment, but barely looked at the clerk. She was looking at herself in all the kaleidoscope of mirrors constructed on a stage-like platform and she was critical but pleased. It had taken three hours in that one store alone to find the ensemble and I was exhausted. Yet, the play was not over. She looked at me, shrugged and said, "Shoes."

But I was done. I could go no more. I told Margaret so and she excused me without as much as a 'goodbye'. Her entire focus was now on the coup de' grace; securing the exact and sensational *chaussure de ville*.

There was a bistro on the corner, and I went in and immediately ordered a whiskey. The bartender poured it over ice without asking me, and that was fine. The liquor was fiery and cold at the same time – it was perfect. The people around me had Gallic faces and they were happy and full of energy and the childlike intensity that was so common among the French. It made me feel better. Whatever they were discussing at the bar, and the tables around me was clearly of great importance to them and the words came rapid-fire from all directions. I took another big sip of the whiskey and this time, it burned more smoothly and I stopped trying to listen for single words or phrases I knew from the conversations and let them all meld into a kind of song and chorus, like the sound of the cicadas on a warm summer night on the farm which often grew so loud I almost felt someone was playing a joke on me. On those summer nights, the bull frogs, coyotes, night herons and owls would often pitch in, and it got pretty crazy. It was like that at the table. I loved the sound of the French language. It was full of emotion and intensity, of human beings expressing the insides of their lives – loves, frustrations, fears and triumphs – and doing so as if it were the last hour on earth. It was a fine, old language.

I wondered then, if I should have a third whiskey. I knew I loved France and the French, but I wondered if I belonged. If not there, though, where? Not back on the farm. That was over. I ordered the third whiskey when the waiter finally turned my way, and then I stopped thinking pretty much altogether and just sat back and listened to the music of the language around me. A flock of elegant rock pigeons dipped over our tables, and then soared off to the side, banked down and fluttered onto the top of a nearby tree. The whiskey burned, and I suddenly knew my story wasn't any good. I shoved the whiskey glass into the middle of the bar, paid the tab, and left.

I walked back to the dress shop, but Margaret had already made her purchases and left. I remembered she had told me earlier she was going to meet friends at The Select. I do not remember much of the walk home except that the wind did not blow, and the sun was warm. I remember the rumbling sound the river made when the brown current hit the bridge pilings and the honk of a taxi that told me I had wandered too far into the street. I did not see the small, dark man shadowing me on the other side of the boulevard, or his black dog, sniffing at the apple crates at the entrances of the *bon marche's* or his instant disinterest when I entered the door to our hotel. I remember the bellman was there, though. "*Ivre mort,*" he said under his breath after seeing me. He came over and said more loudly, "*Il faut manger si on vent rester en vie et en bonne sante.*"

I picked up a little of what he said. "Yes, yes, food would be good. Lamb, with potatoes, *s'il vous plait,*" I said. "*Tres bien,*" he said with a little bow. I did not know why he suddenly had taken a fraternal interest in my welfare, but I did not care right then because I was hungry and the potatoes, especially, sounded good.

He led me to a nice table on the side of the dining room. There were two couples in the room, both sitting at tables. I sat by myself. The roasted potatoes were delicious and after I finished, I went upstairs to bed. During the afternoon I slept soundly. About five o'clock, the door burst open with a loud bang. I bolted upright. It was Margaret, or at least something that looked like her. Her face was swollen and red with anger. She stepped in and threw her bags across the room. It was hard to determine exactly where she was aiming, but one of them made me duck. Her lips were open, and she seemed to be trying to speak, or shout, but no words were coming.

"What is it?" I said. Instinctively, I already knew her rage had to do with me.

"This, Jake! How could you do this to me?" She threw a crumpled ball of yellow paper at my head. I caught it and rolled it open. I had to lay it on the bed and flatten it with the palm of my hand before I could read the small type. It was a cablegram showing a *Scribner's Magazine* logo and letterhead.

"*Story you filed is not acceptable for our publication,*" the cable read. "*Lacking theme and insight. Not what we expected.*"

The cable had been signed by a man named Charles Peach, whom I knew was Margaret's father's right-hand man and the top editor. I sat down on the bed heavily, like a man who had just been belly-punched. The oxygen seemed gone from the room. It was the fear of all fears, the failure of all failures. I was numb.

Margaret, on the other hand, was screaming. "What is

the matter with you? You have embarrassed me in front of my father and all his friends! How could you! You did this on purpose! You wanted to hurt me! Maybe you never had the talent! This is awful! Why didn't you work on this? Why didn't you do it right?"

Those were a lot of questions and except for the one about doing it on purpose, I was already asking myself the same ones. *Why didn't I do it right?*

"We trusted you, Jake! How could you do this to me?" Her face was a mask of anger. She let out a low, gasping growling noise, and then collapsed into a chair and stared at the wall. She sat there like that for a long moment. She didn't move, except one hand was twitching slightly, like the tail of an angry cat. Her eyes were glittering and began moving back and forth, although her head remained still. Then she changed.

"It's okay," she said. "It is okay. It's all okay." Her voice had the sound and feel of a funeral.

I knew it wasn't okay, nor would it ever be okay.

"What are you wearing to the party?" she said.

The change in her mood and the sudden change of subject should have startled me, but it didn't. It wasn't the first time I had experienced that kind of thing from her. I also knew that once she changed the subject, there was no going back to it. Her voice was not unkind, but it was distant, as if she had just transported herself to another reality. Whatever she had decided was done. We would never again discuss the *Scribner's* article.

"What should I wear?" I asked.

Her question about my attire for the party was a serious one.

"Whatever you want."

I knew that meant I'd better choose something she would have chosen for me herself. Relationships often hung in the balance as to the level of ability each had to interpret subtext and understand what the other really meant when they said something else entirely. With Margaret, interpretation was constant, expected, and mandatory.

"Oh, it doesn't matter, we'll talk about it later," she said. "I have to go meet some friends. I'm late." She took her purse and coat and walked quickly out the door, shutting it harder than necessary when she left.

I stared at the door and held onto her anger and reaction for as long as I could, but in the end, it was no use. The reality of the cablegram slammed into me as hard as a freight train. I felt sick. I tried to move, but it was no use. Sweat beaded on my forehead. The air from the window was no good either. My thoughts ricocheted in my head. I had never had a story rejected before, but this was about far more than that. I felt beaten and then I tried to get angry. I shouted out loud: "What the hell do you want, anyway? I wrote a perfectly good guidebook to the gods of our time! My dad would have loved it and so, what the hell, Mr. Peach? Why didn't you love it? What is the matter with you? You people don't know shit! You are all fakes and phonies – sons of nepotism! Sons of bitches!"

After that, I was beat. I sat back down on the couch, shrinking the entire time. I knew I was just howling. I wasn't even saying what I really felt to myself. It felt good to cuss and rant and to cast the editors onto the coals of contempt and kill them in my mind. But I knew the truth and I didn't like it much.

Story you filed is not acceptable for our publication. Lacking theme and insight. Not what we expected.

Theme and insight? They may as well have said "truth," because I knew that was what they meant. They might have thought it a bit dramatic to say it that way, or they might not have used that word because it might have created confusion. For it wasn't truth as in the names, dates and locations of the artists' lives they would have meant, but another kind of truth, the kind I'd been sent to discover, Peach's insight. My head began to hurt. It was balanced in its nasty symmetry with a sudden and powerful stomachache and I lay back on the bed. *Not acceptable for our publication... Not what we expected.* I worked hard to conjure up a last jolt of anger against Mr. Charles Peach and the rest of the world, but I couldn't do it. I lay on the bed and tried not to think at all.

Chapter 20

Sometimes in the evenings, at the darkening end of twilight, before Paris came alive with its legendary lights, Sophie slipped quietly away from the hospital. She made certain no one saw her, and she hurried down the back alleys with her coat collar turned up. She walked for more than a mile in the gloaming, turning every so often to look backwards to make certain she wasn't followed. Her eyes were sharp, and her heart beat rhythms in her chest. She held a large bag in her hand as she hurried down the streets. She thought no one saw her sneak away, but she was wrong. Someone was following her, also careful not to be seen.

By then, Sophie had gained an autonomy of sorts. Most of the doctors typically gave her a wide berth, allowing her to conduct her own kind of healing with patients, without their interference.

However, some of them were inevitably attracted to the strong and lovely nurse, who was always friendly, if a little distant. Two of them in particular, a young, fiery dark-haired surgeon from Reims in the Champagne region of France, and an intelligent, blond, blue-eyed psychiatric doctor from just outside London, were especially intrigued by her beauty, skills and mystery.

Who was this angel and why was she so remote?

Unfortunately for the two suitors, they had similar names. Dr. Guilbert, the surgeon from Reims, and Dr. Gilbert, the Englishman, did not mind until they both began pursuing Sophie at the same time. Then they began to hate the coincidence, and secretly, to despise each other. Someone always seemed to bring up the coincidence in their names, and it was agony for both men.

Sophie did not give either of them much thought at first. She shied away from all attentions and kept her energy focused on her patients, and for a time, she got their names mixed up, too, and simply called both of them Doctor.

They both were determined however, in the way of many men, to outdo each other as much as they were to win over Sophie. Typically, that dichotomous attitude was not a terribly successful strategy for winning a woman's heart, but sometimes passion and ego combined to make a deadly current. The two men were indeed swept away by passion for Sophie, and both meant to win the war between them, that had begun in the hallways of the small, hidden hospital in Paris. This war was never given a name, but it was as pitched and serious as any in any history book. It involved strategies and battles and it had two generals, both of whom vowed they would win at all costs.

"*Enchante' mademoiselle,*" Dr. Guilbert would say to her at every opportunity. He was especially forward in his efforts toward Sophie. He made sure to visit the patients she saw whenever he thought she would be there.

He believed he had the edge over the Englishman

because of his Frenchness. He would fuss over the patients, speaking a flowery form of French not only to show her how concerned he was about the patients' welfare, but also to constantly remind Sophie that he was the clear choice over the Englishman. Whenever she left the room, he followed her immediately, whether or not the patients had gotten a full checkup.

He continually tried to talk to Sophie, and although he was typically clumsy and effuse about it, she was polite and smiled in his direction, but as always, she quickly turned her attention to the patients.

Dr. Guilbert often finished the day with two feelings. On one hand, he felt he was making headway with her, but on the other, he feared she did not consider him in the way he considered her. He usually went to sleep focused on the first feeling, though, and woke up each day encouraged and determined to make more headway with this gentle and glorious creature. There were times when he couldn't remember a single patient's name, as he was completely immersed in Sophie and getting past her secret walls. He was sure he was making headway with her, except late at night when those troubling doubts crept in. He grew angry when they did, shifting blame to the Englishman, whom he suspected of cheating and lying his way into Sophie's favor. He had no proof of that, but every day, his grudge secretly grew.

Dr. Gilbert, on the other hand, was relaxed and liked to joke and have fun with his patients. He was pudgier and did not have Dr. Guilbert's fancy haircut, but he knew all the patients by name. However, like the Frenchman, he did not know how to get past Sophie's cool demeanor. He was more practical and perhaps a bit more honest in his assessment of the situation. At night, alone, he could admit that he did not truly believe he could win Sophie's heart. On the other hand, he was a true Englishman and refused to give up even in the face of seemingly insurmountable odds. Plus, his growing dislike for Guilbert fueled his determination – they had just fought a desperate and catastrophic war together as comrades, but history was history and no Englishman was about to let a Frenchman get the better of him.

Their attentions became so obvious that Sophie could no longer pretend they did not exist, even in her own heart. They caused her great pain. She had locked away nearly all feelings; the bad heat from the smoking ruin of her village, her childhood, and her family had not died down much over time. She had locked that away deep in her soul, so it would not burn all of her down, but the locking away allowed the fire to smolder and the embers to stay bright and dangerous.

Doctors Guilbert and Gilbert were knocking on that door and she had no intention of opening it for them. Maybe someday, she thought, but not now, not for them.

The doctors, however, knew none of that and were not easily discouraged.

"I am thrilled by your repartee with the patients," Dr. Gilbert said to her as they met in the hallway in a coincidental meeting he had carefully planned. He also had planned to use the word 'repartee' to help diminish his rival's advantage in Frenchness.

Sophie could barely understand him because of his thick English accent, but she nodded sweetly and walked on. Dr. Gilbert turned on his heel and caught up with her.

"Say," he said, "I would like to get to know this part

of Paris a smidge better. Is there a chance we can have a spot of tea somewhere this afternoon?"

Sophie didn't drink tea. She didn't particularly like tea.

"Oh, I am so sorry," she said. "I have my afternoon patients. Perhaps another time." She lightly touched his arm and walked away.

For his part, Dr. Gilbert was electrified by her touch and felt he had just gained a distinct advantage over the Frenchman.

Chapter 21

Whenever Sophie left the hospital out the side door at twilight, she always went the same way. She quickly ducked down the alley that ran alongside the back of the hospital. It stank of urine and rotted food. A few big rats gnawed on the fetid meat thrown out, and they barely moved as Sophie hurried by. She was nervous every time, but not so much because of the rats. She knew she would probably end up in jail if anyone at the hospital or the police found out what she was doing. She always wore a man's fedora and glanced furtively around as she walked as quickly as she could down the back streets. She was always relieved when she reached the small, hidden door that led to the basement of a building nearly a mile from the hospital. She had a key and let herself in. There were men in hats inside and they nodded to her and her work began. Sometimes she didn't finish until late in the night.

One rainy afternoon when she was at the hospital, the receptionist found her and gave her a letter that had just come in for her. It was from Cassie's grandmother:

Dear Sophie,

I am increasingly worried about Cassie. She is sad always, and she takes no joy in anything. We have all kinds of animals on the farm, but she doesn't pay attention to any of them. Mostly she sits in her room or underneath an oak tree we have in the pasture. She never gets angry or says a mean thing, but she is without hope or any laughter. She mentions you sometimes. She is as thin as a sheet of this paper. Can you come visit her, please? All our love.

Sophie put the letter down. "Shit," she said. She sat for a long moment. She was terribly afraid for Cassie. Sophie walked to the administration office and made arrangements to get two days off from the hospital. Since she had never taken time off before – in fact, she often volunteered to fill in for other nurses when they traveled – no one fussed over her request.

That night she went home and packed. The next day, she took the northern train that ran within a mile of Cassie's grandparent's farm. It rained that day and Sophie could not see beyond the near buildings on her way north. The train was not full, and she chose an unoccupied bench seat and stared out the window.

What would she say to Cassie? What would she do? Streaks of rain streamed sideways across the window.

The train ran out of the city and into the farmlands. Sophie saw cows grazing in the rail while a few ravens hopped at their feet, and in the far fields great blue herons still hunted the ponds.

Cassie's grandfather was waiting at the train station. He was smiling, but Sophie thought he looked tired and worried.

"We are so happy you have come," he said, at first moving to shake her hand and then giving her an awkward hug. She hugged him back.

"I am sorry I haven't come before, but it's been busy. How is she?"

"Not good. Not good at all. We don't know what to do."

He took her small suitcase and put it in the back of the old truck. They hurried inside the cab as the rain increased.

The truck was one that had served the army six years and it bumped and splashed over the rain-soaked road. A wooden fence, old and sturdy, ran alongside.

Her grandfather said little on the way home. He squinted hard into the rain and constantly wiped the fog off the inside of the windshield with his shirtsleeve. Sophie let him concentrate. There was not much to say, anyway. They were both thinking the same thing.

Ahead, a two-story farmhouse rose out of the rain mist and Sophie saw wood-smoke pouring upward out of a large brick chimney. As they drew closer, she could see a big white fence surrounding a large yard in front of an impressive porch. Above the porch, lights shown out the windows. Cassie's grandmother appeared at the door and ran across the porch, down the stairs and across the yard to meet the truck. Sophie was shocked to see she was crying and nearly hysterical.

Cassie's grandfather and Sophie looked at each other for a moment. His face was the picture of intensity and stress. His mouth came open and he quickly rolled down the window. Cassie's grandmother was sobbing and shouting, and at first, they couldn't make out the words for the rain.

Finally, Sophie understood.

"Cassie's gone! She's gone! I can't find her. Where is she? We have to find her. Oh, something terrible has happened!"

The woman slipped in the mud and fell against the truck.

Cassie's grandfather leaped out, knelt down, and picked

her up. He was old, but still powerful from the work he did every day.

"What are you saying? Where is Cassie? What has happened?"

Sophie raced around the truck, sliding a little in the mud, and reached the two of them. She placed her hands around the grandmother's face and put her own face close.

"It's okay," she said. "We need you to be strong. Take some deep breaths. That's it. Just breathe."

The woman opened her mouth and breathed in deeply as the rain streamed down her face.

"Cassie was strange after you left to pick up Sophie. It was like she had already left this world. I couldn't talk to her. She told me goodbye. I asked her what she was talking about. I told her you were coming up, but she didn't say anything. She just walked out of the room. I thought maybe she was going to change her clothes. But then I couldn't find her. I don't know where she is. I looked everywhere."

Cassie's grandfather ran back to the truck, turned off the engine, grabbed the keys and looked at Sophie.

"Let's go find her," was all he said.

Sophie followed him into the house. They shouted Cassie's name. They opened closets and storage rooms, and went upstairs into the attic, but Cassie was nowhere to be found.

"I'll go out to the old oak tree," the grandfather said.

"I'll check the barns," said Sophie. The grandfather nodded grimly, and they set off into the rain.

The fields between the house and the two barns were saturated with rain and Sophie had a difficult time getting through the deep, slick mud. She took off her shoes. The mud and water were freezing cold. She couldn't see far because of the pelting rain, and soon she gave up holding the hem of her dress out of the mud. She needed both hands to wipe the rain out of her eyes.

The two barns were set off to the southeast of the house. They were shapes in the looming fog, but Sophie kept a true line toward the larger barn. The big oak tree was on the other side of the pasture and the fields and the grandfather disappeared into the mists and fog. She was alone, but she kept struggling forward, her feet making sucking sounds out of the mud with each step.

What would Cassie be doing in the barn? Sophie thought. Maybe one of the animals was sick, but her grandmother said she wasn't paying any attention to them. Sophie was puzzled, but she kept going. It began to rain even harder. She finally reached the large barn. She was drenched and covered in mud of a deep chocolate color. Her stockings were shredded and the harsh wood floor and straw tore at her feet as she went into the barn. The high windows above the loft let some light in and Sophie could see shapes well enough on the barn floor.

"Cassie!" she called. "Cassie, it's Sophie! Where are you? Are you in here? Cassie!"

Her voice slightly echoed through the spaces in the barn and off the upper rafters, but there was no answer. Suddenly, Sophie knew Cassie wasn't in the barn. She shuddered so much she nearly fell to her knees.

She raced to the door, a splinter driving into her heel. There was no time to do anything about it. She stepped quickly back into the mud and rain and tried to run to the other, smaller barn, but the mud was deep. She shouted

Cassie's name as she ran, but the rain and wind drove the words back to her. She pulled her knees forward as fast as she could but trying to run only made things worse. She focused and gained the rhythm of walking with long steps that propelled her the fastest. The smaller barn suddenly loomed in front of her, and she grabbed the door. It wouldn't budge. She pulled with all her weight, but it was locked. Frantic, she moved around the side of the barn until she saw a low window. There was nothing but mud around, so she stripped off her shawl, wrapped it around her fist and without hesitation punched the glass. It shattered, making a tremendous noise, and Sophie nearly fell backward into the mud.

When she regained her balance, she saw the window had broken cleanly and only a few shards were left. She quickly broke them away and laid the shawl over the bottom of the sill. She pulled herself up and turned sideways so she could fit through the window frame. She pulled hard, slid through, and fell to the floor. She looked up. Cassie's body was hanging in the air, silhouetted in gray in the dull light of the window on the other side of the barn. The rope around her neck was tied to a rafter overhead. An overturned chair lay below her feet. Her body was swinging violently from side to side. Sophie froze in shock, but she struggled quickly to her feet. She knew the violent swinging meant Cassie had just jumped off the chair.

Cassie was unconscious. Sophie knew she did not have the strength to hold the girl's legs up to take pressure off the rope, and there was no way to climb to the rafters to get at the knot in the rope, but she had worked on farms during the summers near the Somme. She raced to the wall where the grandfather carefully kept the tools. She quickly found what she needed.

She grabbed a seven-foot scythe, with a curved, sharp, five-foot blade and ran back. She pulled the chair upright and without hesitation swung the scythe in a big arc above Cassie's head. She put all her strength into it.

The bright blade cut cleanly through the rope. Cassie's body fell into Sophie, who threw the scythe to one side and tried to catch Cassie with the other arm. They wobbled on the chair and then crashed to the floor into the hay. Sophie leaped on Cassie like a cat and frantically tore at the rope knot around Cassie's neck.

"Shit, shit, shit!" she yelled, pulling at the rope as hard as she could. Suddenly a pair of big, gnarled hands appeared next to hers' and together, Cassie's grandfather and Sophie loosened the rope and threw it to one side. Sophie immediately held her ear to Cassie's mouth and then took a deep breath and breathed it into the girl's mouth. She did so several times, but there was no movement.

Cassie's grandfather let out a combined gasp and sob. Sophie glanced at him, but quickly turned back to Cassie.

"Breathe!" she screamed. "Breathe, Cassie! You may not go! Breathe, damn it! Now!"

The body remained still.

"She's dead!" the grandfather cried.

"No," said Sophie. "No, she is not dead. She is alive."

Cassie was not breathing. Her face was white.

The rain pounded on the roof like the marching of endless soldiers.

Sophie pushed on Cassie's chest. She leaned down. "Remember the roses, the flowers in the spring! You promised to be here with me to see them! Cassie! Come back!"

A tree limb broke violently outside, making a gunshot sound and crashed into the side of the barn, shaking the walls. Sophie and the grandfather looked toward the gaping hole in the barn where the tree limb stuck through.

When they looked back at Cassie, her eyes were open.

"Hi Sophie," she whispered. "Where are we?"

Sophie burst into tears and put her hands to Cassie's cheeks. "We are right here. Right here! Waiting for the roses to bloom. They won't bloom without you."

Cassie saw her grandfather and looked around.

"It looks like we're in the barn," she said.

Her grandfather let out a quick sound and pressed the back of his gnarled hand to his mouth. Tears were in his eyes.

"Yes," said Sophie, "we are in the barn. It's really nice here this time of year. Cassie, what the hell were you doing?" She picked up the rope, gave Cassie a scolding look like one would give a child, and threw the rope away. She hoped to downplay the terror.

Cassie remembered then and immediately began to cry.

"Yes!" Sophie continued her tactic. "You should cry. And you should apologize. How rude! How are we supposed to see each other and dance when you do something like this?"

Cassie continued to cry, and Sophie moved in and hugged her close. "First of all, are you okay? Does your neck hurt?"

Cassie shook her head.

"Well, that's too bad. It should hurt. Then maybe you'd remember how mean this was."

Cassie stopped crying and looked at Sophie.

"Yes," said Sophie, frowning down at Cassie. "Mean! You expect us to do this all by ourselves? You were just going to leave me, when you are the only friend I have who knows what we've been through? When I love you? When we have so much left to do in our lives? I think that's incredibly rude!"

The grandfather started to move in, not sure of Sophie's tactics, but Cassie sat up and looked at the severed end of the rope and the nearby scythe.

"You saved my life," she said to Sophie.

"Yes."

"Why?"

"That's a good question. Why would I do that?"

Cassie teared up and shook her head.

"You asked where God was. He's in the rain and in the flowers, Cassie. And we can't see those until the spring. Sometimes you have to wait to see the flowers, but they will come. They do come. We will see them together in the spring. All of us."

Cassie's grandfather knelt and helped Cassie to her feet. She turned and hugged him, her face against his chest. She sobbed for several moments, holding him tightly.

"I would say God was in that scythe, too," he said, looking at it on the floor.

Cassie looked at Sophie, her eyes wide. "I don't know how you did that."

Then she saw Sophie's dress. "You are a mess," she said with a sobbing laugh. "Let's go back."

"Yes," Sophie said. "Let's go back."

Outside it was still raining and the rain came into the barn through the hole the tree branch had made. The grandfather knew there was still mending to be done, but somehow, he knew that in time, it would all be okay.

The rain stayed for a few days after that and so did Sophie. They talked and talked about what Cassie had seen in the war and Cassie shared it with her grandparents. They moved on through it together.

On the sunlit morning before Sophie left the farm to take the train back to Paris, she and Cassie sat out on the porch. Cassie had a calico kitten on her lap, while its mother purred contentedly at her side. A couple goats kicked up their heels and practiced butting each other outside the fence and Cassie laughed.

When it was time for Sophie to go, Cassie hugged her goodbye, and they promised to meet again soon. "When the flowers come out," said Cassie.

The air was warm by the time Cassie's grandfather cranked up the old truck and Sophie waved goodbye. The earth seemed to sigh as they rode by and the rain in the fertile fields drained into the ditches on the sides of the road, as it was meant to, and then into the bumping brown streams and, finally, into the broadening torrents of the river.

Chapter 22

The party of the year in Paris was held in a grand ballroom near the Palais Garnier. It was sponsored by *Scribner's Magazine* along with the Parisian Visitor's and Arts Commission, which liked to spend money on lavish affairs.

Robert and Allison were the primary hosts, which was ironic, in my opinion, because they were two of the least lavish people I knew. Somehow, though, they were also perfect for it.

The ballroom was extraordinary. One entered through huge mahogany doors cut from wood that once grew as rugged, big-rooted trees in dense Amazonian rain forests. After being sawed, seasoned and shipped to Europe, they were ornately carved and hinged and hung so one would think they had always been there.

On the night of the party, they were thrown open to the guests, who arrived in taxis, limousines and occasionally, gilded horse-drawn carriages. The styles that night varied and soared. The week before, Allison had shared with Margaret the importance of style. "The difference between fashion and style," she said, "is that fashion is when people notice the clothes, and style is when you notice the person."

Some of the flappers wore bejeweled headbands or cloche

hats and climbed from the carriages flashing long, lithe legs under short silky skirts. Others came in flowing, graceful gowns, white gloves past the elbows; and deeply blushed cheeks. Their hair was up in expansive and expensive clips. Mysterious curls were allowed to slip out and down.

It was a time and place where women easily powered everything in the room – a setting that was becoming far more common in 1925. Diamonds, emeralds, gold, and silver glittered on wrists, necks, and fingers. The handbags were small and glinting and hung from long, ropy straps. Most impressive, though, were the shoes. The shoes were the show of shows with pieces of art fitted onto every woman's feet. There were black heels with golden straps and ornate floral patterns, smashing midnight-blue heels with hand-painted designs, and red ones with a thousand silver sequins exploding across the front.

Overall, it was a feast, a glittering orgy of sight, scent and wondrously hardening fantasy for the men. Every woman was beguiling and flashing, and each held the depthless mystery of desire under the dazzling, shimmering lights of the crystal chandeliers.

Some of the men wore wide trousers called Oxford bags, and many sported single-breasted vests under double-breasted coats. A few wore the Panama hats they might have worn on the streets, but others preferred the fancier homburgs and those whose wives had taught them style wore silk top hats that bespoke of power, money and social standing. Perhaps that was why the wives smiled sweetly when they chose their husbands' party clothes. It was a circular thing that left the men thinking they were in charge.

For men, the rage was short tuxedos, with black-worsted swallow-tailed coats, trimmed in satin and matching pants.

Some showed off with subtle shiny black ribbons of satin which ran down to polished black shoes. They wore spotless white shirts with black bow ties and although most of the men looked more or less alike, they were nevertheless, smashing. Champagne poured out of large fountains. There were wondrous creations of chocolate, strawberries and sugared nuts at various tables and the giant chandeliers spun gold and silver light across the growing crowd.

A band playing Cole Porter and all the other latest rages swung into action on the big stage at the far end of the room. The crowd kept coming through the open mahogany doors, an endless stream of intoxicatingly beautiful people and swaying gowns. Fringe on the flappers swung enticingly, the men rumbled boisterous greetings, and the champagne flowed freely. It was definitely the party of the season. It was the last place I wanted to be.

Earlier, Margaret had come back to the hotel room and disappeared for some time into the bedroom until she emerged in the figure-hugging gown the color of lilacs, with hair shimmering like minted gold coins and eyes that promised a man everything. I complimented her, and she nodded absently. We walked to the lift and rode silently down to the lobby. The bellman was there. He said nothing when he saw us. I thought it was strange that he did not compliment Margaret. Everyone complimented her all night, but he bowed slightly to us and did not say anything. Margaret ignored him, and for a moment, I felt as if something had happened between them to make them silent enemies. I did not know what.

We walked out of the hotel to a taxi, with Margaret turning heads on the street. She was mindful of the attention and smiled slightly like a general smiling over her troops. Who was to say that the outcomes of the battlefields of women have had less impact on human history than those of men? Who was to say there were fewer casualties? I nearly tripped and fell into the street as I followed Margaret into the taxi. I was still fussing with my bow tie, which did not want to stay tied.

The ride to the Boulevard des Italiens seemed interminably long. It was normally a time for couples to excitedly talk in restrained conspiratorial tones about who would be there and exactly why it *wouldn't* be the great event of the year, followed by a quick agreement that it would be a great event, nevertheless. It was a time for the man to give the woman a small kiss on the cheek, with her turning away slightly so as not to smudge the perfect applications of paint and powder. Nothing like that happened between Margaret and me, but I couldn't help looking at her. She was flawless. She stared out the window, as she had done when we first arrived in Paris.

We arrived fashionably late, and the party was swinging when we walked in. Robert and Allison were at the door to meet us. Allison was beautiful in a simple, elegant white gown by Elsa Schiaparelli. I did not know who Elsa Schiaparelli was, but Margaret made a point of complimenting Allison on it. Allison's smile was radiant, and I thought then that she was the most beautiful woman in the room. Robert was in a tuxedo and he grasped my hand heartily and smiled broadly. If he knew of my rejection by the magazine, he did not show it, and I knew I would always be in debt to him for that. He hugged Margaret carefully, so he would not put even the smallest wrinkle in the dress. He was good at that.

"I am glad you came!" he said sincerely. "This wouldn't have been a party without you."

I looked around. "There are hundreds of people here."

"I know." He laughed. "But I think you two will be the most interesting in the room tonight!"

I noticed Allison's smile lessen for a moment, but she recovered and nodded, and Robert beamed at us. "Go now! Mingle. Try the champagne, but, don't get lost. There are people here I want to introduce you to."

Robert bowed theatrically to us and turned back to the next guests coming through the door.

Margaret clasped my arm as we made our way into the crowd, but it was a perfunctory move. Ahead, people were dancing, and someone thrust flutes of champagne into our hands. There was elegance everywhere, and everyone seemed to be pouring in like glittering diamonds down a sizing chute onto a silver floor.

The noise levels grew, the band played louder, and there wasn't anything left to do but dance, which I could do, although I wasn't any great shakes at it, but Margaret was. She could Charleston so that people usually stopped to watch her and so she did, and they did, and I moved as best as I could outside the circle. I put the champagne down – no matter how dry it was, it always tasted too sweet to me – and drank a glass of cold, clean water.

I lost Margaret then, in a whirl of Charlestons and quick-step boogies and young men who crowded around her. I could see flashes of her lavender dress for a while, swirling and flying as she moved with a man's arm around her waist, and then she disappeared completely. I found it a relief to be alone, if one could be alone in a room full of hundreds of mad partygoers bent on having a good time. Perhaps that was one of the easiest places to feel alone, though, and I took a deep breath, tried to fix my bowtie, and thought for a quick moment that this was the other side of the moon from Kansas. Then a large hand grabbed my shoulder and spun me around. It was the writer, and he had a huge grin on his face, as if he knew I was trying to escape but was having little luck.

"Here," he said, offering me a drink from his flask. I was surprised at the offer, but I took it and drank. The whiskey was good. I tried to bring my hand down, but he held my elbow up and said, "More! There's more! We won't run out. I know where Robert stores the bottles." I didn't argue and downed another long fiery slug. Sometimes whiskey could be a very reasonable thing.

"Paris is the city of cities, the city of men, where the beating of Europe's heart is felt," he said. He looked at me and raised his eyebrows. He was testing me.

"Easy," I said. "Victor Hugo."

"Bravo!" he shouted, clapping me on the back. "Then one more! 'There is never any ending to Paris and the memory of each person who has lived in it differs from that of any other'."

I thought about it, but he had me. I shook my head.

"Hello then! You are a good man! Most bastards would guess just to show how fucking smart they are," he roared over the noise. "That son of a bitch was me! Some day that will be in my book, if you don't steal it first!" He laughed. Then he took the flask and finished it.

"Come on!" he shouted. "I'll show you where the bottles are."

We got up, and he shouldered his way through the crowd as we covered the huge dance floor and soon climbed a long, burnished wooden stairway and swung around to a landing. Below was the party, spread out and moving, with beautiful faces everywhere and in nearly every gloved hand a glass of champagne. I couldn't see Margaret, but I saw Robert and Allison still near the door. Guests were still arriving. Everywhere there was movement and color and a star-studded magnificence spread across the crowd.

The writer ignored the sight and hustled up the stairs with athletic bounds. I noticed that although he sported a slight limp, he still moved so fast I could barely keep up.

"Here," he said, and he opened a door near the back of the hallway. It opened up to a huge room containing rows of wine racks that nearly reached the ceiling. There were dozens of them. The writer ignored the bottles of wine and went off to the side to a series of lower wooden racks. The whiskey was stored there, each bottle on its side, label up. He took a bottle, opened it, grabbed a funnel from one of the racks, placed it in the mouth of the flask and poured the rich, brown liquid into it. It poured smoothly and then he capped off the flask. When he was done, he lifted the whiskey bottle by the neck and drank.

We sat on the edge of a table and drank the whiskey. "Remember when I told you that things don't turn out like you expect?"

"Yes." I could tell, in part, that he was still testing me.

"It's all about what you do after," he said. "You don't know a damn thing about a person until you see what they do after. They can't hide what they do then. That's how you really know about them. Do you sail?"

"No."

"Hmm," he said. "You should sail if you can. A man learns to do what he has to do on the sea. The sea doesn't fucking care, and things don't ever turn out like you expect.

You should learn to sail, and then you'll know what I mean. War does the same thing, but you can't always depend on having one of those around when you need one."

I laughed.

After a little while, we started downstairs. He continued to talk as we went. "One other thing. Don't pay any attention to editors, critics or any other bastards who have never written anything themselves."

I was stunned. Did he know? *He must know. Shit!* Did everybody know?

"They are sons of bitches, too," he said. "Don't let them bother you. Don't even read what they write about you. None of them would ever say that to your face. Whatever they won't say to your face you shouldn't listen to."

We reached the bottom of the stairs and then we were out on the dance floor. Robert Meeshon suddenly appeared, took both our arms, and led us out of the way of the dancers. "Gentlemen!" he said with a wide grin. "I see you found the whiskey. I just wish I had been there with you."

The writer laughed. "You have one less bottle than before."

"And there will be less than that before the night is through," said Robert. "Come on. I want Jake to meet some people."

I didn't know why Robert wanted to do that. I was feeling done for. I didn't have any purpose in Paris anymore. My work simply wasn't acceptable. I might have started to feel sorry for myself but being around those two bursting men suddenly turned my self-pity into anger.

"Sons a' bitches!" I said out loud and the other two men laughed.

"That's it!" the writer said. "That's what they are and that's what the whole world is sometimes." He swung an imaginary haymaker in the air and accidentally knocked a lady's hat off. She turned, startled, but laughed delightedly when she saw who it was.

"My apologies mademoiselle," he said gallantly, and with a flare he picked up her hat, gave it back, and then gave her a kiss. She kissed him back, and that was when we lost him because Robert pulled me on through the crowd. We reached a long table where a number of elegantly dressed men and women were laughing and drinking wine. I recognized some of them, including the man nearest us, who was of medium height, and had a slight build and wavy, fair hair. At his side was a woman with wide, attractive features. There was something unsettling about the way she looked at me, as though I had already been judged and found wanting. She was obviously drunk, and I thought he might have been, too, but he carried it easily, like a man used to drinking.

"Do we want to know this man?" the slightly built writer said about me.

I wasn't insulted, I was amazed. The man was a great writer, maybe the greatest so far. Robert laughed and introduced us. I shook his hand. He had a strong grip. I knew he had written one of the finest books ever written in the English language. Of all of them there in Paris, the slightly built and slightly effected man, was the biggest god of all to me. He was huge and powerful in his writing, yet in person, he appeared practically dainty. *Things don't turn out like you expect.*

Robert introduced me to others that night. The wide-eyed bearded poet, whose hair stuck up in all directions, turned out not to be the stereotypical wild man I thought.

Instead, he seemed the sanest of them all. Later in the night, he tried to point out to me those whom he said, with some contempt, were Communists, but that meant little to me. I didn't care. I was not particularly fond of Communists after the cold-blooded murder of the czar and his family, but I didn't attribute that horror to an ideology. Leaders who emerged after civil wars were most often little more than skillful and narcissistic architects of death and oppression, no matter what ideology they claimed. The poet seemed a decent man. My father always had believed that a man who was not a decent man would never achieve anything of lasting value in life. Nor would he ever be properly rewarded. Maybe it was my father's need to believe in a just God that led to such an aggressive belief about 'decency'. You were in for a fight if you said anything different. It was simply too bitter for him to believe that those who were not decent could prosper. Or maybe it was out of his fear that the arrogant, self-serving and cowardly bastards of the world were actually going to take control somehow and win in the end. For my father, it was too much to consider. *Only great men do great things.* In the back of that melody were hard rhythms and harsh choruses that sang of perfection – a song I had heard since I was a child.

I liked him, at that moment, and most of his poetry seemed sane to me. Later, however, the poet sent my father's belief crashing to the ground when he sided with the devil himself in the next world war.

Robert took me around the table, and I met more poets and writers, including one a novelist from Mississippi. He had a black mustache, smoked a pipe and was no taller than 5'5", but he was a 'literary giant', according to a few New York editors. They called him brilliant and hoisted him among the gods. He was getting quite drunk when I met him, even as I was becoming less drunk, and that was rarely a smooth crossing. He scarcely acknowledged me, although I did hear him say, with his southern drawl, "Civilization begins with distillation," as he sipped the mint julips, made especially for him at Robert Meeshon's order to the catering staff. I wondered how he would have fared with the Communists. Not well at all, I thought. The southern writer and his new form would not have found an appreciative audience among the Communists and would not have been called brilliant. He most likely would have been shot. There in Paris, though, people were safe, for now, and could say and drink and do as they pleased. It truly was where Europe's heartbeat could be felt. Right now, though, it was my heartbeat I was worried about. I hadn't seen Margaret for more than an hour.

Chapter 23

Outside the pavilion, Sophie was returning to the hospital. She often worked evening shifts, taking care of the patients who could not sleep for the nightmares. The noise and lights from the party burst onto the sidewalk, and for a moment, she stopped walking and peered inside the open doors. It was hard to distinguish anything specific. The party was a moving mass of color – high flutes full of champagne, dresses, gowns, hats, tuxedos, music, dancing everywhere, some somber men talking off to the side, and one couple slipping away up the stairs. It looked like wonderful fun.

For a long moment, Sophie felt a deep sadness that she wasn't part of it. Since the Englishman and the war, she hadn't allowed herself to go out much, to be social, dance or do things romantic. She let her guard down when looking at the party, and it felt joyous and wonderful. She wanted to dance with a handsome man, drink champagne and forget everything for a least a night. But her patients were waiting for her, and she knew she had to move on, down the street, which now seemed much darker and colder than it had before. It was hard to turn her back on the lights, warmth, and gaiety of the pavilion. She started to cry as she walked. She wiped her eyes with her scarf and got mad at herself for being emotional. That was still dangerous for her. It was a cold relief when she could no longer hear the music. Still, her whole body shuddered, and a surprising number of tears came again around the corner. She angrily wiped them away again with her scarf and tried hard to focus on the bright barge lights reflecting off the river.

***

I looked for Margaret, a lavender flow on the dance floor perhaps, but I had no luck and Robert soon motioned for me to come over to a table set up off to the side of the pavilion. On top of the table, huge arrangements of pink and black African flowers towered over the champagne bottles that sat in buckets of ice like tilted soldiers. Tuxedoed waiters stood, one hand behind their backs, and poured as soon as they saw a glass raised, which seemed a perpetual blur. Robert was standing near the slightly built novelist and his beautiful and very drunk, wife. She had bobbed hair and had an air of something I hadn't identified yet. I had never seen anyone quite like her. Sometimes she seemed to focus on a person, and everything seemed normal, except maybe the intensity of her focus. She was slightly built, like her husband, but they commanded a huge presence around the table. Even the poet and the painter gave way to them, such was the quality and beauty of his book. As I looked at her, she seemed to go into some kind of trance, as though she were someone else, someplace else, and we were all being left behind. That was okay with me. I didn't think I wanted to go where she was, but she was definitely the queen of the table.

I watched as she and her husband drank and talked with theatrical flairs but not to each other or even to the same audience. A group of elegants was listening to her on one side, and a mixed group of men and women was listening to him in the opposite direction. It was as if a competitive audition was going on and they were both giving it their best. Most of the others sat giving rapt attention to the couple, except the painter, who looked restless. One got the feeling he was always restless, and deep down, an instinct told me I didn't trust or like him much. But it didn't matter, there was so much going on, and all of those observations took place in parts of seconds. Allison came up on my shoulder and pressed my arm. I turned, but instead of giving me her customary smile, she looked almost sad. She seemed somewhat anxious at the same time.

"How are you?" she asked, and I sensed she wanted to say something else.

"I'm having a fine time," I said. "You look beautiful."

She smiled quickly.

"I think you are beautiful, too. You are the most handsome man in the room."

Her words surprised me. She wasn't flirting, more like throwing a floating ring to a drowning man. I felt it and appreciated it but didn't understand it yet.

We stood and watched the show for a moment. The dancers began to expand across the floor, and even our group was not immune. One by one, they left and paired-off to move to the smooth music from the big band. Silk gowns swept across the dark wood floor, hugging shapely derrieres. Everywhere were jeweled necks and long tapered white gloves on slender arms held out by tuxedoed men with combed-back hair. Many of the men wore white gloves as well and danced and moved their partners with bent knees and graceful swings. They danced close during the Vienna waltz and kisses were frequently stolen or given. Couples bent and swayed as the music played, and the lights glittered. It was a huge vibrating play in Paris, and Allison had swept up one of the bearded poets and led him onto the dance floor where he showed a surprising skill. They laughed and moved beautifully together. Robert was dancing with a woman I didn't know, and the slightly built writer and his wife had paired off with different dance partners. Both could dance well, but the flapper wife insisted on doing the Charleston even though no one else was, and she sometimes kicked those waltzing around her. She didn't seem to care. It would be years before she was finally taken to a mental asylum, where she would die in a fire, and he would lose his ability to write, and the whole thing would collapse and be reduced to an immense alcoholic tragedy of lost talent. Right then, though, they were still flying high in Paris, and everyone was still young and beautiful.

Outside, the river ran dark and strong but inside, the wine was clear and good, and the hunger and desire of the dancers ran high and hot. I caught myself watching most of the time but twice, I was asked out onto the floor and enjoyed myself a bit, though my mind was elsewhere. I still couldn't find Margaret, and I could see at least half the pavilion from my vantage point. No lavender gown. Between sets, I decided to walk the rest of the way around to see if I could find her. It was a slow walk, with people stopping now to enjoy more wine and sparkling water. They were talking, women were fanning themselves and some of the men were opening their collars. I kept walking but even after several minutes still did not see her.

At last, I came back to the table. Allison and the others were still there, but I didn't see Robert. I then saw the thin writer lying on the floor. His wife was passed out on two chairs nearby. Nearly everyone else around them had had too much champagne, too, although Allison was fine. I saw that the writer's pale blue eyes were wide open. I moved closer and was immediately sorry I had.

"Do you like me?" the thin writer shouted to everyone, slurring his words. "I mean it! Do any of you really like me?"

Two inebriated young women were on their knees around him and they cooed, kissed him and murmured things, but he pushed them both away and shouted his question again. I backed away, wishing like anything that I hadn't heard him, or seen it. I'd been around drunk men before, plenty of them, and I didn't like the ones who became foul, or those whom the alcohol gave the ridiculous and ill-fated courage to fight, but this was something completely different. It was a terrifying destruction, a disastrous crumbling, like the horrifying sight I'd witnessed as a child of a huge and beautiful house being pulled over a cliff into the ugly maw of a sinkhole. Each part of the house had cracked and fallen over the edge, one after the other, and each had shattered with a heartbreaking sound. You couldn't stop it. After the final piece of the house caught the grip of quick gravity, I'd crept to the edge and saw a porcupine-like heap of splintered and shattered wood and plasterboard. Then I'd tried to picture the elegant house as it was before and couldn't do it.

I backpedaled, stumbling away, as if the drunk writer presented a danger. His wife was limp and white as a ghost, and I could see no movement in her at all. She looked dead, but she was only dead drunk. I did not want to see that, either. I turned and left. There was nothing left for me, and I needed to find Margaret. I pushed through the crowd, ignoring the protests and spilled wine. I wasn't aware of much, just the urge to move and keep moving. I was finally satisfied that Margaret was not on the floor. I checked with the two white-coated ushers at the door, and they shook their heads; no woman matching Margaret's description had left through the front door.

Finally, I found myself at the bottom of the stairway. I had a bad feeling and I didn't want to climb it again, but it was the only place left. There were other rooms upstairs I knew, besides the one full of Robert's whiskey. I climbed the stairs one-by-one, and the noise from the crowd seemed to fade. I remember the burnished and gleaming wood of the stairs, the curve of the bannister, the landing at the top, and the long corridor lit by a single chandelier. I walked past the room with the whiskey and wasn't tempted. I walked on, and my feet seemed to move by themselves over the gleaming wooden floor as I headed toward the light at the end of the hallway. There were tall doors on either side, with white porcelain handles. Some were open, and some were not. The first door I walked by was open slightly and I could see a couple inside. They were standing in a tight embrace, kissing in the half-light, the lights of Paris blinking through the window behind them. She wore a white gown. I walked on.

The next two doors were shut, and I could hear nothing from inside. I kept going, pretending not to know where I was going or why. Finally, I came to a larger door, and it was also half-open and there was light coming from the window. I stepped inside. There was a large bed, and on it were two people. The woman's gown was pulled down from the top, so it gathered around her waist. Her breasts were naked and pale in the light of the window, and he was kissing them. Her head was tilted back so I could not see her face, only her long blonde hair. I recognized him immediately as the painter. Then I saw the purple gown, and then I saw her face as she brought her head down and pulled her delicate hand through the painter's black hair that flopped over his face and her breasts.

Then Margaret saw me. Her hand stopped, but she didn't otherwise move. She just looked at me, her face immutable. She did not show surprise, embarrassment, or anger. I thought for a strange moment she was going to shrug, but she did not, although I saw a look of inevitability in her face. She also did not stop the painter from doing what he was doing. He did not know I was there.

Just like that, our time was past. All we had, and all we had done was past. Our present was past, and the future I had thought we might have had was past. She didn't make a move except to turn her head slightly as if to give me a final glimpse of her perfect profile, the perfect woman in the lights of Paris.

I stood there for a moment, feeling like an outsider, and strangely, no anger welled up inside me, nor was there any other sharp emotion. It was the opposite. I went completely numb. I felt nothing at all. It was all gone. Empty. Empty. Empty. I had no emotion, no action to take. I could have whipped the painter with ease, but I did not blame him, and I did not feel any anger. I looked at her face and saw it all disappear and then there was nothing left.

Downstairs, the party was still going on, but I didn't seem to hear the music, and I don't remember walking out the big doors into the cold. Allison saw me walking out and pushed hard through the crowd to get to my side. She surely knew about Margaret and the painter. She tried to talk me into staying at the party, and she hugged me and asked me if I was all right. I merely nodded, kissed her on the cheek and left. She turned and disappeared quickly into the crowd. I suspected she had gone to try to find Robert to help convince me to stay.

I left before they could return. It was cold outside, and it started to rain a little bit. In a few minutes, I was far from the party, and it began to rain in hard little drops, and the small, hard drops irritated me. The rain was the only thing I could feel, and I realized I hated those irritating raindrops. I got angry at them, and I clenched my fists and shouted something at the clouds, wishing I could fight the rain and inside, an ember of rage glowed.

I walked down Avenue de l' Opéra past the upscale hotels and their well-dressed doormen, none sported the singularly tight coat of our doorman, and I reached the bridges, and it began to rain even harder. Thunder rumbled down from the west, and I walked across the bridge and went down toward the river. I came around the corner where the quay began, and I suddenly stopped. The rain was cold, and a thick fog was creeping down the far banks of the river, and what had happened at the pavilion was just beginning to penetrate my brain.

I still kept myself from seeing her with him, but overall, a crush was beginning to squeeze my head and chest and I sucked in as much air as I could. I remembered the flask the writer had given me, and I pulled it out of my coat pocket. The whiskey was hot, but the rain cooled it fast. I finished it. The fog grew closer. I was on a small dock now, and I was suddenly aware of the river, running dark and swift, only feet from where I stood. The fog was moving over from the far side of the river, and the rain sheets made a perfect splash pattern across the top of the water. On my side of the river the streetlights still shone silver and gold. They led to the heart of the city and to the scent of midnight bread being baked now so it would be ready for the early morning, and back at the party, the champagne still flowed and the two met together in the perfect circle of Paris. Paris was all I had left. I stood leaning against a stone wall, and I knew I was drunk and that the river was rising. I took a step toward it.

Behind me, from a dark opening in the bank, a black dog came sniffing out, hunting, serious and nose-down. Behind him, his small dark master, as intent as the hunting dog, moved quietly through the shadows toward me. I heard nothing but the river. I leaned heavily back against one of the thick barrels that sat on top of the wall. I smelled the apples inside, and where one of the barrels was partly cracked open, I could see the apples inside. I watched the river, wondering how it would feel to step off the bank and sink to the bottom. Would it be cold? Would there be light down there? Would it lead to a city? A different civilization? What was down there? I walked unsteadily toward the black current.

Then, from the side, I felt a bump and stumbled for a moment. Hands fumbled in my coat. I instantly thought back to the careening car and the short thief stealing the man's wallet. I knew mine had just been lifted. Quicker than the thief expected, I shot my hand out and grabbed his arm.

I spun around. Dark eyes gleamed at me. It was the same pickpocket I had seen days ago with Margaret, when the car tipped over. I wasn't surprised. I hit him quickly with a short left. He staggered back but didn't go down. His balance was good, and he was quick. He leaped backward, his face impassive but focused. Blood came from his nose. I closed on him quickly and struck him again with a short left jab. He dodged, so I hit him only a glancing blow, but I followed it with a straight right that had enough power and anger behind it that had it landed, it would have done damage. However, the thief, who had been in tight places before, was lightning fast, and the whiskey had slowed me. He dodged to my right at the last moment, and my fist barely grazed his head. Quick as a fox, he jumped up onto the wall, and ripped one of the broken oak staves loose from the apple barrel. I expected him to run from me, but he had nowhere to go. He was trapped, which he realized quicker than I did. He jumped down at me and dodged to my right. I turned too slowly. He closed the distance and slammed the wood plank into my face. I saw it coming but couldn't get out of the way. I felt it land across my eyes, stars exploded in my brain, and then it all went black.

Chapter 24

The night was quiet at the hospital, and Sophie had already checked her patients. She gave herself a moment to sit in one of the soft chairs by the window of a room set off to the side for the nurses. She could see out over the river and the rooftops to the lights of the city beyond, where the party was with the music and laughter.

Did she miss that? Did she miss having a man wrap his hands around her waist, dancing, clinking champagne glasses, and having someone look at her as though she were the only person in the world?

The night sky for her, was still filled with longing. In the past few years, she had stayed in the present moment as best she could. Sometimes, though, the deep sadness snuck in. She didn't try to fight it or deny what had happened to her parents. Most often, she brought out her easel and canvas, sat on her balcony and painted until the pain subsided. Still, the pain of her parents' death had eased only slightly for Sophie, and it was still fresh when she first saw the stars each night.

Her father had been tall, handsome and strict. But he'd loved to read stories with Sophie on his lap at night when she was young, and she remembered how the fire in the fireplace had popped and sparkled as though it were a part of the story, as the orchestra was to an opera. He'd read stories of kings, queens, princes and princesses and ordinary people, too. Her father quickly noticed her rapt attention when he talked about animals, so more often than not, his stories had woven themselves around beautiful mares, brave stallions, meadows, mountains and magical waterfalls. Sometimes there had been headstrong goats, and faithful dogs and mischievous cats in there too.

Sophie's mother had been an intelligent and pretty woman, with a passionate love of philosophy and history. Her parents had been Americans from New York who had moved to France as an adventure. They'd fallen in love with the Somme River Valley, happy with how different it was from New York.

They'd encouraged their daughter – Sophie's mother – to grow up fearless and outspoken, although, at the same time, her father had constantly worried about her future. What proper Frenchman in the late 1800s wanted a wife who could argue politics better than he could? He'd been relieved when Sophie's father, a young attorney, fell madly in love with her and didn't care about politics. His father, Sophie's grandfather, had been the mayor of Flers since anyone could remember and had been rumored (although there was a good chance he himself might have helped fuel the rumor), to have been descended from ancient Gallic kings and queens, who once ruled the lands near the peaceful River Somme. But Sophie's father had not cared about politics. He'd loved literature and he and Sophie's mother had fit together with ease and delight. He'd worked long hours and sometimes that became an issue between them, especially after Sophie was born. He could be stiff, formal and sometimes stubborn, but there never had been any doubt – for the rest of their lives – that they loved each other fully.

For her part, Sophie's mother never had lost her *passion ardente* for politics, but raising Sophie and tending to their modest estate, which her father had given them as a wedding present, had kept her busy. Their land had been on a southeast bend in the Somme River, and the soil had been rich, and the crops had grown tall and healthy. They'd prospered and, in the evenings, especially the longer twilights in late summer, they'd eaten dinner outside on the fine and ancient rock terrace and watched the French sunset spread orange and sometimes golden and sapphire sparkles across the top of the slow-moving river. A short time later, the river and the farmlands around it had been filled with tens of thousands of bodies and become the largest graveyard in Europe.

"Let's go inside, my love," her father would eventually say to her mother as the sun fell below the far trees. She would nod and kiss him on the neck, and they would all take the dishes and silverware inside. She and her mother would wash them while her father prepared a fire in the fireplace.

Sometimes Sophie would shiver with delight during those times. When the last of the plates were washed and dried, her mother would pat her on the back and Sophie would run to her father, who by then was in his chair with a steaming cup of coffee. Sophie would climb up and settle and her father would always look down in mock surprise.

"What have we here, a little mouse?" he would say.

"*S'il vous plait*," Sophie would say. "Read to this little mouse. She is ready for a story."

He would laugh and then sigh, as if that weren't exactly what he wanted to do. He would open the book with an exaggerated flair, and he would always say, "Now, let me see. Where were we?"

That always would make Sophie giggle and she would fill him in on the last thing he had read to her the night before. He would nod sagely, adjust his reading glasses and then begin. She snuggled her head against his chest.

After school, Sophie often had played with her friends, but she would come inside in time to catch the late afternoon light in her mother's art studio. They often had used oil paint, pencils, pastels and red chalk to honor her mother's muse, Suzanne Valadon. Her mother had painted with bold strokes and colors, which had delighted Sophie, and once, when she was older, her mother had painted a couple making love – with the woman looking at the man as an object of desire. Sophie had been amazed, and she and her mother had become partners in wonderfully scandalous and liberating elements of the painting, which they'd skillfully hidden from Sophie's father. There was a limit to what you could expect from men, after all.

Sophie's mother had sensed early what was coming. She'd read the newspapers and listened to the talk, and by 1913, when Sophie was fourteen, she'd shared her fears with her husband. Sophie had heard the concern in her mother's voice and her father's thoughtful replies. He'd respected his wife's opinion, but he'd had a law practice and a farming estate and leaving Europe altogether, as his wife was asking, had seemed impossible. Sophie often had heard them talking about it. "Europe is headed for something evil," her mother had told her father. "I fear we will be in the center of it all, right here in this village. We should go to New York. America will be safe, and Sophie will adjust quickly."

Sophie's father had not disputed her suggestions, but

neither had he acted on them. He had lived in and around Flers all his life and it might not have been within his capabilities to leave it. When the war started, few had been able to get visas, so they'd been pinned to the land north of the river and the fighting erupted all around them. None were able to get out. The roads were blocked virtually overnight with tanks and trucks. Railways had been commandeered by the military. Her parents, like everyone in the village, had been terrified and confused. How could the war have come so fast? The bombs that killed them were the result of one of the first big battles along the Somme River. So many people were killed the top brass on both sides hadn't bothered counting. Later, the bombing deaths of the villagers were blamed on poor mapping by the Germans and the hot gun barrels. No one knew exactly how many civilians had perished, and not many cared.

Sometimes, after a long day at the hospital, Sophie would drop into a soft chair in her small office on the first floor. Exhausted, she'd close her eyes, and sometimes she could hear her father's voice reading to her about kings, queens, and heroic mares and stallions who did not die in wars but lived in beautiful places where the sun shone through the trees. Then she would think of the secrets she'd shared with her mother, and she would smile.

She was just beginning to relax, when suddenly, there was a great deal of noise in the doorway of the hospital.

Chapter 25

I don't remember waking up to pain, but I remember the darkness well.

"He's alive," I heard a man say.

"He's a lucky bastard," another man answered.

Then one of the voices was right in my ear. "Hold on. We're going to pick you up. It will probably hurt like hell."

Hands gripped my shoulders and legs. It did hurt like hell, and I would have fought them, but I couldn't see them for the darkness. I was dizzy, trying to stay conscious. I touched my fingers to the throbbing in my forehead and my hand came away wet.

"You're bleeding," one of the men said. "A little guy told us he saw you fall off the rock ledge."

"Said you fell and hit your head," the other man said. "You're lucky he found us."

I must have passed out because the next thing I knew I was lying flat on my back in what felt like a bed. It was still dark. I was annoyed that wherever they had taken me still had the lights turned off. I could feel a cold cloth wipe the blood off my face.

Why would they do that in the dark?

I tried to talk, but nothing intelligible came out. A female hand gently touched my shoulder and pushed me back down onto the bed.

I grabbed her arm.

"Who the hell are you? Where am I?"

"You are in the hospital," the female voice said. "You've had a bad fall."

"Fall? What are you talking about?"

"By the river. You were found down by the quay. You were unconscious. Were you walking?"

"Fall? Is that what that little son of a bitch said? He tried to rob me."

"Be quiet now," a male voice commanded. "We will sort all this out later. I am Dr. Bertrand, and I need for you to be quiet. You have a bad wound and I must do what I can with it."

"In the dark?" I said angrily. "What the hell are you doing? Get away from me!" I struggled, but they held me down.

"I was afraid of this," the doctor said. "It is not dark in this room. It's that you cannot see. Your optic nerve is damaged. That is why you see only darkness. You are blind. Now, stop moving."

I sank back on the bed. I couldn't comprehend his words. I tried to put all the pieces together, but nothing fit. For a moment, I was back in the pavilion and I saw lights and dancers, and then I saw Margaret in the bed with the painter, her gown askew. I believed he was lying because I seemed to have my eyes open and I could see it all.

"Bastard!" I screamed. "Liar!" In that moment, I was as

terrified and lost as I had ever been. I had no idea where I was, who was trying to wound me with that monstrous lie or why I was there. Was it a nightmare? I had to get out of it. I struggled and then sank back down and forced myself to wake up. I blinked and blinked again and again, but the nightmare wouldn't end, and I couldn't wake up. I couldn't see no matter what I did. Then a wild panic set in. I drew up and laughed and shouted shrilly and madly. What a frightening dream! I would laugh at it and then wake up and conquer it. I would laugh at them, all of them!

They held me down. I still couldn't see who it was. I struggled until the morphine they injected into my arm took away my strength, and I lay back again. Slowly and in a haze of the drug, I began to realize that the creeping terror of the truth was in those hands I could feel on my head and face. They would not go away, no matter how hard I tried to make them. The terrible hands of the doctor kept moving and hurting and they wouldn't let me wake up. It became increasingly and terrifyingly clear that I was already awake. No matter how wide I tried to open my eyes and how often I tried to blink away the darkness, there was not a shred of light in the room. Bandages were being placed over my forehead and my eyes, and I finally froze like a man deep in a cavern of ice and stopped struggling.

Then I felt a warm, light, sweet touch on my face, and I heard her voice: "I am Sophie. *Vous allez être bien.* I am here with you."

Chapter 26

For the next few hours, Sophie's voice was all there was for me. She spoke to me in English – soothing words to distract me as the doctor continued sewing stitches into my face and head. The morphine helped, but it still hurt like hell. The sound of her voice seemed to bring colors with it; silver and a soft rose color I often had seen on the Kansas plains just before daybreak. I could also see the yellow of the sun. Her presence alone kept me from plunging into total madness and I lay back, feeling her hand in mine. My senses leaped to it. Her hand was small but strong and calm. My connection to sanity. Then the morphine really kicked in, and I was gone again.

Sophie did not tell me until much later that she did not think I would live out the night. I had lost a great deal of blood, and only the fact that I'd been found quickly and rushed to the hospital had saved me from bleeding out in the darkness on the riverbank. She had seen worse injuries during the war, but my wound was bad, and she stayed by my side throughout the night. The doctor stayed nearby too.

Although she never let her feelings show, she told me later my situation greatly disturbed and depressed her. The war had been over for six years, yet she watched as men still battled each other, the delicate art of peace seemingly unattainable, out of reach like fluttering butterflies above the mustard fields. It saddened and angered her, but she tended to me carefully. I slept through the first day and most of the second, but on the night of the second, I woke. It was dark and at no other time was I as acutely aware that I could not see. It was silent in the room, although I sensed someone might be there with me.

"Monsieur, you are awake," Sophie said.

She did not ask me how I was feeling, and I was glad because I probably would have uttered a stream of profanities for which I always would have had regrets. Instead, I grunted and said something like, "Ummm."

I heard a rustle and then felt her hand in mine again.

"The Inspector of Police was here and wanted to talk to you yesterday, but we sent him away," she said. "He said he knows you. He said he will be back, but not for a while. The doctor is very persuasive when he wants to be."

For the first time, I tried to remember the exact details of what had happened.

"How long have I been here?"

"Two days. You have had other visitors. We sent them away, too."

"Good," I said. "I do not want to see them."

I always sensed the scent of flowers whenever Sophie was around. I didn't know what kind, but whenever she left, the stiff medical smells of the hospital closed in afterward.

She was silent.

"I need to talk to the doctor. Is he here?"

Sophie went out and got the doctor, and I heard him

sigh and sit heavily in a chair by my hospital bed.

"*Bonjour*, monsieur," Bertrand said.

My questions came out in a rush. I demanded to know everything about my condition.

"Your head and face are healing," the doctor said. "But they will take time."

I started to interrupt, but his voice stopped my assault.

"It is your eyes you want to know about. I know that. You have had a great blow and injury to your head and then a concussion."

"I damn well already know that!" I grabbed the bedrail and nearly wrenched it loose.

The doctor ignored me. "You have damage to your eyes, no doubt. We don't know how much. It could be a complete retinal detachment. The retina is a thin layer of tissue lining the inside of the back of your eye. Its role is to help turn the images entering your eye into signals that go to the brain through the optic nerve. That nerve may have been damaged or severed. Also, in head traumas like yours, blood can flow into the retinas of both eyes, and the blood pools, and that finally tears the retinas loose. In either case, I am sorry there is nothing we can do."

I could not grasp what he'd said.

"In either case, you will not recover your sight."

Not recover? My mind became a wall of defense. His words refused to register in my brain.

The doctor was silent. He knew most new trauma patients went through a struggle of denial, defiance and then anger. It was better than the alternative. Suicide watches were put on the others.

Sophie broke in. "Doctor, what if it is vitreous?"

"No!" he said icily. "We will not discuss that." He was not going to have his diagnosis questioned even slightly. "That is not likely and will give him hope when there is no hope. It's better that he knows and faces the truth."

I heard him stand up and walk out. The door shut hard behind him.

A heavy silence hung between Sophie and me. She was angry at the doctor's response, but I was reeling from what he'd just said. Sophie must have seen my dismay, and she came quickly over to the bed. She pulled a chair over and took my hand.

"There is always hope," she said. "I have seen it. I have seen miracles, and you don't need one. You just need to heal. Don't listen because listening might make him right, and he is wrong. I know it. So do you!"

She spoke like a witchdoctor, a shaman, a healer. I do not recall exactly what else she said, but I used what she'd said before as a shield against all the terrors that wanted to take me over. I was given a strong sedative and it was morning before I awoke.

I woke to darkness and became sick. I was sick for the next three days. The wound in my head was deep, and infections tried to get in. It was very bad for a while. I lived in a world of blackness, and I lingered in shock and denial. I focused only when I heard Sophie's voice and felt her touch as she changed the dressing on my bandages and talked to me in honest tones as I lay in the darkness. I tried to maintain my anger toward the thief, the doctor, and the world in general because it acted as a barrier against the terror.

Blindness was, at first, a narrowing thing. My mind refused to think beyond the present moment; neither past nor future was allowed to have an existence. I survived from second-to-second, until the seconds turned into longer measures of time, and then I lost track of them, and there was no difference between night and day. There was only the time when Sophie was in the room and the time when she was not. I didn't think about anything; my mind was blank, and I focused all my attention on listening to everything I could hear. Every sound was amplified. I could hear the clinking of glasses and dishes on the carts as the orderlies brought food to the other patients, and then brought back empty dishes. I sometimes heard muffled voices in the hallway, whether angels, gargoyles or devils were speaking, I did not know. Sometimes I imagined them all. I could hear birds sometimes, that was how I knew it was daytime. They cooed and trilled, and sometimes I heard the movement and rush as they swept off the ledge above my window and beat their wings on their way to their mysterious rendezvous. Sophie said they were doves that lived on the roof, overlooking Paris. White doves. I came to covet the sound of their wings more than any other.

As the days and then more than a week went by, I began to imagine I could hear ants, cockroaches, and spiders crawling around my room and sometimes over the bed. I had no fear of them. I welcomed their company. They came without judgment or prejudice and with no knowledge of the giant gods in the clouds, how corn rows had to be perfect, or what a blind man's life would be like. They just went about their business and they did not care. I loved them for that. I listened for them, and I began talking to them. Nothing complicated, of course. A simple "How do you do?" sufficed, and they went on straight about their business. One time,

Sophie came into the room silently because she thought I was sleeping and heard me talking.

"Talk to me too," she said.

So, we talked. I told her about the odd and awful rhythms of panic and terror that seemed to come and go at their own pace through my head.

"I can't stop them by ignoring them and they won't yet let you have whiskey," I said. Sophie did not laugh.

"This might seem easy for me to say and very hard for you to do, but you must always confront your fears. Do not run from them," she said over and over. "It's the only way."

It sounded like a terrible cliché to me and at first I ignored her advice. But she kept saying it, and I soon realized all I had were fears and what she was saying was all that was important in those early days at the hospital.

Chapter 27

Meanwhile, outside my room, the mini dramas within the hospital were heating up. During the time Sophie had been gone to Cassie's and during the days I had been at the hospital, doctors Guilbert and Gilbert had not diminished their personal war. They had continued to bicker and argue, never about Sophie directly, as that would have put them at odds with the hospital administrator if he'd heard about it. But they fought over almost everything else.

I even heard about it sequestered away in my room. An orderly told me about them and even gossiped that my name had come up between the two feuding doctors. They were aware that Sophie was spending a lot of time with me, but they decided I was not a threat; however, each of them was to each other. They wrote my situation off as Sophie's usual concern for patients. Plus, the gossipy orderly said the two doctors had decided it was absurd to them that she would ever enjoy the company of a man who was blind, obviously crazy and perhaps worst of all, a journalist.

Like the rest of the staff, they weren't sure what to do with Sophie on a professional basis. She was superb at her job, and the doctors were content with her as long as they continued to take credit for her ability to heal patients.

Increasingly, though, she had become more businesslike and decisive to the point where she was once again annoying the doctors. Her decisions were inevitably in favor of the patients' health, but still. In the past years, she had been the peacemaker and they all relied on her to make things run smoothly. Now she had changed, and most didn't like the change. It caused the entire hospital to be a bit on edge.

The doctors Gilbert and Guilbert did not sense the unease. They were too busy plotting maneuvers against each other. One day Dr. Gilbert could not find his charts on some of his lesser-injured patients, and ultimately had to write them all over again. The originals were in Dr. Guilbert's trash bins at his apartment, a mile away. Dr. Guilbert could not find his stethoscope, which he proudly wore every day, even to the corner market, and more than once, to church. Suddenly, it was gone. He searched everywhere and could not find it. Mortified, he had to order a new one, and oddly, there were none in the hospital, so he had to wait several days for one to be shipped to him from another hospital. At first, he wouldn't come out of his office, but then a horrible thought grew in his brain, and the grinning Englishman was at the center of it. The Celtic bastard had stolen his stethoscope! His immediate reaction was to march to the Englishman's office and hit him right in his smug, Churchill nose. It seemed the perfect solution. Dr. Guilbert jumped up and strode toward the door, but two thoughts stopped him. First, he would undoubtedly be fired from the hospital if he struck another doctor. That was sobering enough, but it was the second thought that made him sit back down again. He had missed the war, as being a doctor had allowed him to stay at home in Paris and had never fought or hit another man with his fist. Thinking hard about that, he remembered he had taken target practice with the militia behind the medical school auditorium once. He remembered himself as a pretty fair shot. He wondered if he should get a gun. He could shoot a gun. He thought about it but decided to exhaust all other tactics first. If nothing else worked, then he might find a gun, although he had no real idea how one went about finding a revolver. A rifle, he decided, would be too much to handle. He put it on his list of things to do.

Dr. Gilbert did not think about guns, but his anger toward the Frenchman was at a high pitch. He was sure now that he was in love with Sophie and that the other man was standing squarely in his way. Neither had actually even taken her out to lunch or for a glass of wine, but they were locked in a combat that they could not escape. Sophie took their breath away and ignited their dreams every day. The thought of losing her to the other was unbearable.

One rainy day, Dr. Guilbert took the brave step of bringing Sophie a gift. It was a bottle of Dom Perignon champagne. He was from the Champagne region, and he wanted to make the most of it with Sophie.

Dr. Gilbert saw the bottle before Dr. Guilbert could get to Sophie.

"What?" the Englishman bellowed. "Why are you bringing that imposter of a wine in here?"

Dr. Guilbert stopped immediately and turned quickly toward the Englishman. His face was already red.

"Imposter? What in the devil's own hell are you talking about, sir?"

The Englishman laughed scornfully. It sounded forced and faintly ridiculous.

"Everyone know; champagne was created by the English.

The statement brought the room to a halt. The orderlies and nurses stopped doing their duties and stood up in shock, as if the moon had reversed course or flowers had started growing upside down. The hospital's only security guard, who had never had a reason to pull his gun in the six years he had been there, was stunned. His jaw dropped a bit. He took a step backward.

"That is the most damned preposterous, obstreperous nonsense I've ever heard!" Dr. Guilbert stammered. He was more stunned than angry, but then a large vein in his neck began to pulse. "You are the scandalous, illiterate son of a fisherman."

Dr. Gilbert laughed scornfully again. "You arrogant frog. Your pompous Dom Perignon didn't make champagne. He stole it from an English doctor from Gloucester, Christopher Merret, who wrote the first recipe twenty damn years before you people pretended to stumble upon it. Liars and imposters!"

Like almost everyone else on the first floor, Sophie heard the commotion and walked out into the foyer. The two doctors were now squared off and glaring at each other. Neither really cared about champagne, neither regularly drank it, but the confrontation had been simmering hotly while Sophie was gone. The coming battle was inevitable; the result irreversible.

Dr. Guilbert cursed richly in French, and then said in English, "You are deliberately trying to provoke me. Monsieur Perignon was a Benedictine monk and a cellar master and as everyone knows, he bottled the first magnum in the abbey's vineyard in the autumn of 1697. You are the imposter! English are all imposters!"

"Aha!" shouted Dr. Gilbert, waving his finger dramatically in the air. "Now the cat is out of the bag! Aha!"

Sophie grew furious. Their shouting was clearly upsetting the patients. Some of them could not leave their rooms but had their doors cracked open to see what was going on. I could not hear the ruckus since I was upstairs, but later, an orderly filled me in on what happened next.

"This is absurd. You are absurd!" the Frenchman roared. "What you say about Monsieur Perignon is blasphemous and a declaration of war!"

"What would you know of war?" the Englishman shouted back. "You French talk, and that's all. You talk, talk, talk! Like big-nosed, squawking fowl! You are cowards – all of you – especially you!"

Had they been unarmed, the confrontation, no matter how heated, might have just become a matter of amusement to those who witnessed it.

However, the full bottle of Dom Perignon Champagne in Dr. Guilbert's hand was a formidable weapon. Swung by an angry suitor, it could have killed as easily and surely as a bullet or bayonet. His grip slowly went to the neck of the bottle.

What happened next happened so fast there were many renderings of it in the followings months and years to come by those who saw it. I was later given the following account.

Dr. Guilbert, shaking with rage, stepped forward toward Dr. Gilbert, whose lips were curled in defiance. The Englishman then made fists of his hands and stepped forward too. They stood and glared at each other for a moment. The Englishman pulled back his pudgy fist, swung at the Frenchman, and connected with a *thack* on the Frenchman's jaw. It wasn't much of a blow, but it sent Dr. Guilbert over the edge. He growled and swung around behind him and then up, so the bottle was above his head. There was no doubt in any witness's mind that he was intent on bringing it down with full force on the Englishman's head. The entire crowd of injured patients, nurses, and doctors in the foray looked on with incredulity. The security officer stood to Sophie's right, in wooden disbelief. Only Sophie moved as Dr. Guilbert swung the bottle down with full force. She swiftly pulled the pistol out of the officer's holster, took a brief aim, and fired.

The collision of sounds was deafening. The gun went off, the bottle exploded, and the two doctors dropped to the floor like rag dolls. Some onlookers screamed when they saw the two combatants covered in a reddish liquid. For a moment, some thought Sophie had shot them both. They were writhing on the floor with their hands over their heads. Both were yelling for help. Slowly, witnesses realized they were covered not in blood but in Dom Perignon's finest. Sophie's aim had been perfect. The bullet struck the center of the bottle, and the wine had drenched everybody. There were stifled cries and frantic murmurs, and some people were still hiding behind the furniture, but most eyes were on Sophie. She was shaking the gun in the air, her eyes smoky and fierce.

"Idiots!" she yelled at the doctors, who both looked up from the floor in sheepish wonder. They were soaked with champagne but otherwise unhurt. "You are all idiots!"

With that, she turned and stalked out of the room and down the corridor with the gun still in her hand, but now dangling at her side. The security guard made no move to get it back.

Chapter 28

The story of Sophie's marksmanship raced throughout the hospital, and it wasn't long before I heard at least four full accounts, each slightly different. Sophie, who apparently was the least shaken up by the event, did not go home for the day but maintained her rounds. She'd never had patients so compliant or doctors more courteous. She rather liked the effect.

When she came into my room, I couldn't help but smile, and then laugh. It was an intense relief to my current situation.

"So, you know," she said. "I wonder which version you heard. The one where I mowed down everyone in the neighborhood with a cannon?"

"Yes, that was one," I said. "No prisoners either."

"Well, good," she said. "If this is what it takes to make some of these doctors realize they are not children, then I am not sorry at all."

I laughed again. "It may take more than that. How are you with grenades?"

She made a noise of exasperation, and I knew the conversation about the champagne shooting was over for now.

Surprisingly, she came and took my hand.

"Let's talk about something else," she said. "How are the cockroaches?"

"Busy," I said. "You would not believe what goes on in their lives. Their schedules make us look like pikers. It's why they have so many legs. You can tell the males from the females, though."

"Oh?" said Sophie, a bit surprised.

"Yes, the females have a heavier step. It's all the pistols they pack."

I felt her fist hit my arm.

"That's not funny."

I couldn't help but laugh again, and she hit me again, softer this time.

During the following days, I looked forward more than anything to my conversations with her. We did not talk about how I'd been injured or why, but about small things, which had become the important things and sometimes she held my hand. We talked about the bad food in the hospital, and I said I would give anything for a fresh sandwich and a glass of whiskey. She laughed and said she would see what she could do.

I asked her how she spelled her name, and why it wasn't 'Sophia'. She said her father had not liked that "a" at the end of Sophia because it sounded Italian, and they had always fought the Italians. Although he liked Italians personally, and had drunk many glasses of wine with Italians, he had wanted her name to be French.

She laughed when she told the story and I loved the sound of her laughter. For the first time, I squeezed her hand back, and then a heartbeat later, she pulled it away and let go. Before long, though, she laid her hand back on top of mine and then we stopped talking, and a little nervous silence bound us together. She recovered by fussing with my bandages, and then she put a hot towel around my cheeks and chin.

After a few moments, she took the towel off, brushed cream onto my face, pulled out a big razor and shaved me. She was careful and delicate, and the razor felt like a caressing hand. It took my breath away. Before that, I had never really thought about shaving. With her doing it, though, I felt every stroke, every pressure, and each tiny movement across my face and neck. Strangely, I did not try to visualize what she looked like during that time. I simply felt, heard and sensed her, and her touch was all there was in the universe when she was there. At other times, when she was gone, I listened intently to the chatter of the small birds outside, the rattle of the dishes in the hallway, and in the quiet times, the scurry of ants as they trekked single file across the floor on their way toward an unknown ant place. I was thrilled they were so alive and had a definite purpose as they moved about. I borrowed greedily from that energy and purpose – from that guileless existence – and I was sure they did not care that I stole from them.

Dr. Bertrand was my only other visitor besides the orderlies who brought the abysmal meals on their rattling carts, and he did not come often. He was usually abrupt and aloof. He moved quickly and said little. I was grateful for that because when he talked, it was inevitably to deliver gloomy predictions about my eyesight and my future. Even when it seemed he was trying to be encouraging, it came out bad. An orderly always removed my dressing before the doctor came in, so he could inspect my wound. He checked the long line of stitches that pulled my skin and face back together, and I could hear his pencil scratch across paper. Then he would stand and say, in French, "You are progressing," and then he'd leave.

Progressing toward what? I always asked myself, and I always felt worse whenever he came.

At night, I sometimes thought about suicide. I laughed bitterly to myself over the fact that it would be impossible to pull off a decent suicide because I could not even see the window, nor could I see the cabinets where there might have been knives. There wasn't much else to choose from because they wouldn't let me near the pills or anything else I might use.

One night, after a particularly dreary visit from Dr. Bertrand, I did try to find the window. I thought jumping might be my only chance. As I climbed carefully and quietly out of bed, I wondered again which floor I was on. No one had told me since I arrived. The thought that I might be on the first floor and throw myself out the window only to fall four or five feet suddenly occurred to me. Or I could have been six stories up and fallen through the night like a bat without wings and then died, bloody, on the street. It did not matter in the end, because when I tried to move away from the bed, I grew dizzy and fell to the floor. I hit my head pretty hard and passed out on the tile. I woke up at some time, but I was too weak to climb back into bed and eventually fell asleep down there.

Early in the morning, Sophie came in and found me. *"Qu'est-ce que tu fais?"* she shouted, and that woke me up. It was the first time I'd heard anger in her voice.

"Sleeping," I said.

She responded with a rapid-fire launch of words that I later learned was an excellent usage and intricate linkage of angry French profanities. She grabbed me under my shoulders, and I thought she was going to help me into the bed. Instead, with surprising strength, she shook me. My head bounced off the mattress, and I groaned. *"Bon!"* she said, but then she calmed down and helped me into bed. She was still not happy, though.

As the morning went on and her anger faded, she told me about Cassie, and we talked for nearly an hour. She lingered in my room all morning, and as she changed my bandage, she also talked about her home for the first time. Taking her time, she shared the things that one remembered about one's childhood, and my room suddenly seemed warm.

"The village was ancient and beautiful," she said in English. "We lived on a street with plenty of shade from the *chenes* – big oak trees – and there were so many flowers everywhere in the spring and autumn. There was a small schoolhouse, and all the children in the village went there. It was a happy place for me. I loved school and the books and all the dreaming you could do when you read them."

I loved the sound of her voice. I listened and tried hard to imagine the village.

She described each season, including what it looked like and smelled like. She said the air in deep fall was as sharp as the edge of a razor and clean, and it felt good on her skin, and the water in the creek was clear and good. Her father kept a cow and chickens, and they were healthy and full of energy. The children at school were happiest in the spring and summers and spent as much time outdoors as they could before the cold winter shut things down.

She told me about the ancient stone church where her father said God lived. She went into the old church most often with her parents on Sundays, but sometimes she went by herself as she got older, and it smelled of oak, old polish and incense. She touched my shoulder and laughed as she said this, and then she whispered that she secretly did not like the smell of the incense and did not think it made the church any closer to God. She liked the scent of the wild lavender flowers outside the church, though, and the way the green grape vines smelled right after the rain.

Sophie's stories were the highlight of my day, and although I did not try again to throw myself out the window after that, I still wondered how far down it was to the street, especially when the doctor came. My wound was healing slowly – far too slowly as far as I was concerned, but Dr. Bertrand continued to tell me it was normal.

"You are not stronger than nature," he said. "Even Americans are not stronger than nature." He sniffed when he said that, and he slammed the door when he left.

As the days went by, Sophie talked often about her village, and I began to realize it was not just for my sake. She seemed to need to talk about it and remember it, and to make people come alive again. I came to know her mother and father through her stories, and one time, she brought a book to my room and read a passage to me that her father had read to her on his lap in front of the fire, before it was all gone. It was in French, and I didn't understand most of it, but Sophie did not go on long once she realized the extent of my illiteracy.

"He loved poetry," she said, making a transition to the shorter passages for my sake. It was difficult to sit on my bed and focus on poetry because my desire for her had risen like a rocket. What I really wanted to do with her had nothing at all to do with paper, books, poets, or even ideas. I actually groaned out loud, and then to cover, I quickly reached up to my head as though that's where the pain was.

"Are you all right?" she said, quickly coming over and placing her hand gently on the other side of my face.

"Hmm, I think so," I said. "It was just a sudden thing." I wasn't trying to trick her. I was just embarrassed, and my problem wasn't subsiding at all with her standing next to me like that. She kissed me gently on the top of my head and then walked back to her chair.

"My father would only read me the sweet parts of poems," she said. "You know, most poets are dark, brooding types, but once in a while, they would write something warm and wonderful, and my father would always find it."

"Such as?"

"Oh, he loved Apollinaire - in part, I suppose, because he was a French poet. He would argue with anyone who tried to say Apollinaire was not French. My father claimed him as French, and that was that."

She laughed.

"And what did Apollinaire have to say about it?"

"Here is one little thing my father would read to me:

Under the Mirabeau flows the Seine
And there I watched you play among the flowers
Hours and hours

And now that we are home by the fire
I will remember it until I retire."

I laughed. "That's not how the poem goes."

Surprisingly, she did not laugh back.

"I know," she said. "My father usually made up parts of the poem so I would like it and so it would come out fine. He loved poetry when he read it to himself, but he did not like the fact that poets were championed because of their dark pessimism. He was at war with most poetry, but he loved it just the same."

"Give me another example."

"Okay, this one he changed only a little.

A bird drank a dew
From a convenient grass.
And then hopped sideways to the wall
To let a beetle pass.

I hesitated for a moment, not sure if I should do what I was about to do.

"Jesus," I said, and then I quoted the first stanza of the poem aloud.

A bird came down the walk:
He did not know I saw
He bit an angleworm in halves
And ate the fellow raw.

Sophie looked at me in amazement. "You know Emily Dickinson?"

"She was required reading for farm boys in Kansas," I said.

She laughed a little but, after a while, I heard her start to cry quietly.

I wasn't sure what to do. I didn't think her tears were about me. My instincts told me she was thinking about her father and mother, and the war, and all that had happened. I knew then she hadn't dealt with any of it, and being a man, I immediately wanted to fix it for her, but I knew I could not help much except to listen. The real fix had to come from her.

"Is this for your father?" I asked.

"No, this is because of my father!" she said with sudden anger. "Don't you see? He only read me the sweet, naïve parts and left out the other. *Mirabeau Bridge* is about loss, not flowers. It goes:

> *Love vanishes like the water's flow*
> *Love vanishes*
> *How life is slow*
> *And how Hope lives blow-by-blow.*

"The damn bird only let the beetle go by because he had already killed and torn the worm in half. My father didn't like reality. He ran from it, but he didn't run from the one thing he should have to save our family; the war."

I heard her cry even harder, but she kept going.

"That's it! Had he not skipped the real parts of the poems he might have been able to see what was coming. He could have known how evil people can be and he could have saved my mother."

She broke down.

"He couldn't face the truth and that killed my family."

I was silent for a moment longer. I sensed she did not believe what she had just said but needed a reason not to.

"Your father was just reading to his little girl," I said. "Like all fathers who love their daughters. I am sure he knew what was coming – we all did. Even in America. The question no one knew the answer to, was where. No one knew the answer to that. I'm sure your father would have escaped to Paris had he known, but Paris is where most people thought the war would start. He was just trying to keep you safe in the safest place he knew – your home."

I felt her suddenly sit on the bed next to me. Her hand was shaking when she took my hand.

"But he didn't want to admit to himself the bad truths about people."

"Who does? But most of us aren't unlucky enough to live on the Somme River in 1916."

"It was luck then?"

"Yes, unbelievably bad luck, and that is all. Your father was not at fault for the insanity of that. If men were all like him, there would be such peace that generals would be out of work forever."

She cried and laughed at the same time. "Yes, and maybe they all would have to become farmers."

"Yes, but we farmers aren't all bad."

"No," she said, and she kissed me on the cheek. "You know that is not what I meant. Besides, you are not a farmer anymore."

"I don't know what I am anymore," I said, and I was immediately sorry I'd said it. We had just crested a hill, and now I was tumbling us down again.

I was struggling to find some way back, when she said, "You are a man, Jake. A very good and kind man. There is no greater thing to be than that."

I shed a tear or two when she said that. Luckily, my tears were absorbed in the gauze, and I thought Sophie couldn't see them.

"My father used to read me Tolstoy when I wouldn't go to sleep at night," she said. "That usually did it. But I remember one thing he wrote, and my father repeated it to me many times."

"What was that?"

"He wrote, 'If you want to be happy, be'. Isn't that splendid?"

"Yes. That is splendid."

For the first time since my fight with the little thief, some light seemed to creep into my soul and the reason was sitting right next to me. I thought about telling her that, but sometimes that kind of eager confession could be too much, and I did not tell her until later.

Sophie began humming a tune and I could tell she was dancing lightly across the room. I listened and could feel her movements. The thought and image of her movements in my mind stirred me and that was good. She laughed like a waterfall for a moment, and then came and hugged me about the shoulders and I felt her hair, her face, the softness of her breasts, and her angel's breath on my neck. For the rest of that night I did not worry about the window, nor did I ever after that.

Chapter 29

Early one morning, Dr. Bertrand came in with a definite purpose. I had learned to tell who opened my door and even what each person wanted by the sound and energy applied. Sophie's entrance was always smooth and easy, without pretense or rush. The orderlies almost always banged into the door first, shoving it open with their carts and dishes. They were usually nice, and I never minded when they came in. Dr. Bertrand's entrance always seemed to be unnecessarily abrupt and have a thin odor of antiseptic to it, and I never liked it. He rarely shared information with me except to say I should adjust to my new lack of sight as quickly as possible. I had a vague picture of him in my mind: dark, covered eyes and a mustache and small beard hiding the rest of his face. I didn't know why I saw him that way in my head. I never asked Sophie what he looked like and she never mentioned it.

"Visitors have come to the hospital several times to see you, but I did not believe you were ready to receive them," he told me that morning. "I still do not believe you are ready. But I fear someone will tell you about them – he meant Sophie – so I am telling you now."

His words penetrated me like a slow sword thrust. My small, fragile, sightless, world with no past and no future, suddenly and irrevocably collapsed around me. The other world came in quickly and I could not keep it out. The past came with it, and suddenly, I was standing in a torrent of pictures and sounds, of my father and mother and all those I had known before. Even Margaret. I could not escape. I fought for air, and it all got damned confusing. I lay back on the bed.

"The man said his name is Meeshon and that you are friends," the doctor said. "You must tell your friends that you cannot see, nor will you ever. Tell your friends that and let them console you. Rely on them and your other friends, and then you can get on with it."

The doctor, satisfied he had done his duty, turned and walked out the door. I didn't listen to him. I was dodging and tumbling down a hill into oblivion, into a darkness more without feature or form than before. I lay facing the wall for a long time, and I did not realize Sophie was there until she touched my hand.

"Jake, I have something to say, and you must promise never to repeat it," she whispered. I didn't move. "I know what the doctor just told you, and I know how you must be feeling, or at least I can guess and feel that for a second, but you must hear me. Do not believe what he says. Do not despair. There is a reason for you to hope."

For the next several minutes, Sophie carefully told me what she had held back before. "I would be fired and never hired again in Paris if the doctor knew I was telling you this," she whispered. "But I trust you, so we are trusting each other. The doctor is wrong. He would hardly accept it if a man was to ever question him, but a woman saying he is wrong would drive him into a frightful, vengeful fury. So, I have not brought it up until now. But now you must listen.

I have seen many more injuries in the war than he has, and I have studied this." She hesitated for a moment, and when she spoke again, I could hear that she was smiling. "Plus, you have called me a witch doctor, and that is what I am. What I am going to tell you is true."

I was listening.

"What you have is called a vitreous hemorrhage," she said. "Each person's eye has in it something that you Americans might call like jam or jelly. It is like something a child might put on a croissant, and sometimes when you have a wound, that is the right word, no? A wound?"

I said it was.

"A wound then can break the blood vessels, and then the blood goes into your eyes and gets caught in this jam and jelly, and it blocks all the light from the sun and the lights, and you can't see but darkness all the time. I think this is what has happened to your eyes.

"And so?" I was impatient.

"In time Jake – and I have seen this – it will go away, and your eyes will heal, she said. "Then you will see all the world again. I believe that this good thing will happen to you."

It took a moment for her words to sink in. I hadn't allowed myself to think about it one way or another. The doctor's visit a moment ago had ripped a huge hole in my psyche, and Sophie knew it. That was why she'd chosen this moment. I feared believing her, and I feared not believing her. I must have shown signs of stress because Sophie immediately came closer. She stroked my face and said, "Remember, vitreous hemorrhage. It sounds like a town in Poland or something." She giggled, and it made me feel better.

I took a deep breath and tried to relax. "A town in Poland," I said. "I am to put my faith in a town in Poland. Okay then. No one I know of has fought longer or more valiantly for their freedom than Poland. I am glad you chose them. If you say so, I will."

After that, I tried. But between my visitors, the doctor and Sophie's hope, the future had snuck in and pinned me against the wall like a flaring cobra.

Chapter 30

I recognized Robert Meeshon's voice immediately. "Hello, Jake. It looks like you are taking a break," he said.

I forced a laugh. "Hello, Robert. I'd tell you it is nice to see you and that you look fabulous, but as you can see, I fucking can't see a damn thing." I was shocked at my own vitriol. If he was surprised, I could not hear it in his voice. Good old Robert.

"Hell of a bandage," he said. "Must have been quite a thump. We've missed you. Man, you gave us quite a scare."

"I just wanted to see Paris by night," I said. "Hell of a city."

"We haven't caught the son of a bitch who did this, but Jean-Claude is investigating, and we will get him," said Robert. "You can be assured."

"How is Allison?"

"She is fine, Jake. She was worried sick about you. She came down here twice, but your doctor wouldn't let us in. He's something, Jake."

"Yeah, he's something all right."

"I couldn't get much out of him, but he said that gash on your head is healing. Wouldn't say how much longer you get to be in the Ritz here."

"The Ritz." I laughed. "You should try the food. Puts the Select to shame."

"Seriously, Jake, you can come stay with us to recuperate."

It was a hell of an invitation, but it hurt sharply and deeply because I still wasn't prepared to think about specifics of my future.

"I would bump into your walls," I said.

"Our walls can take it. Allison would love to take care of you."

Take care of me. It was supposed to be comforting, but it felt like freezing rain.

I didn't say anything, which was rude I guess, but it was the moment and Robert understood. He gripped me on the shoulder. "When it's time then. We will be there. There is plenty of room. You can learn to write again -- maybe better than ever! Is there anything I can do?"

"No. You are kind. Please thank Allison. I don't know what will happen."

Robert did not know what to say next, so he gripped me again on the shoulder, wished me good luck, and left. I felt concussed, as if a shell had just exploded near my head. It was a hell of a thing.

That afternoon, I lay in bed, and images of the past slowly crept in. I thought about Margaret, but I could not get the picture of her and the painter out of my head, so I put her aside as much as I could, and then I realized there was nothing I wanted to have in my head, so I concentrated on listening for the ants and the big cockroaches. I liked the big ones because I could really hear them. Sometimes I knew the orderlies were trying to kill the cockroaches, and I got upset and asked them to stop. They promised they would, but I knew they wouldn't.

Days and finally weeks went by after that. Robert and Allison came by a few times and we talked. They were unfailing in their support, and I always felt worse when they went away. Sophie kept me alive during that time. She talked, more freely each time, about her past and her family and told me I must someday write something that some father might read to his daughter at night. She said that several times.

Sophie came to my room almost every day, sometimes more than once. She never stopped believing in my healing. I let her hope be mine, and she caressed my face sometimes and let me touch hers. It was amazing to touch a face I'd never seen. When I was younger, I had seen a blind boy about eight years old excitedly touching a statue in the park, and he'd correctly labeled all of the carved and chiseled-out animals he could see with his fingers: "That's a dog! Lying down! And this one is a tiger crouching!" He'd been right every time.

"It is as natural for him to collect information from the world with his fingers as it is for you to do it with your eyes," his teacher had told me. "Blindness is not death. It is life collected differently. All his passions are still there, and it is up to him to engage them, just like us."

I'd admired that boy then, and now I wondered if I would ever have the courage he had.

Touching Sophie when I could not see her was one of the most remarkable things I had ever experienced. She sat patiently as I traced her face with my fingers. To me, it was a splendid face. Her forehead was like porcelain, and I felt her hair; silk and satin. She closed her eyes so I could run my fingertips over them, and I felt life and energy and something more too -- something I couldn't identify. When I mentioned it, she shrank back and seemed angry at me for a moment. I went on without saying anything and ran my fingers slowly over her high, soft, cheekbones and the skin felt like the golden linings of clouds.

I said that and she laughed, and then I felt her warm lips and mouth. My heart shouted. I had never felt anything more satisfying in my complete being than that touch of her lips. She neither pursed her lips nor pulled them away but kept them true and steady, and I had never had such a feeling and did not know how to describe it to her when she asked. "Maybe I will someday become a writer, when I can find the right words," I said.

She broke into a smile with my fingers still on her lips and said, "Maybe soon."

The next morning my door opened, and this time I wasn't sure who'd opened it. It was a different energy that came into my room, one I wasn't sure I liked. "Bonjour," said a man's voice I didn't recognize.

"Hello."

"My name is François, and I am here to talk about how it is going to be in the world for you as a blind man. We call it the reinstitution process, and I am here to teach you about it."

I would have punched him if I'd known where he was in the room. "Reinstitution process?" I said. "You sound like you're coming to train a dog or an idiot."

"Ah, anger is usually the first thing we encounter," said Francois.

"It could have been something else," I said.

"Good," he said. "You are going to need a fighting spirit."

"Jesus," I said.

"We have several steps to take," said Francois. "It's best if we take them together. You will need to listen carefully because your life will never be the same. You will be like a child, and it won't be easy. I can make it easier for you. You'll have to pay attention and do everything we say. First, you must begin to accept that you will never see again and that your life will be one of a sightless person."

I swung my fist hard through the air, meaning to crush the sound of those words. I hit nothing. Francois had smartly positioned himself out of haymaker range. "I can see you are one of those who will make trouble for himself," he said. "Some never adjust. I'll do my best with you, though." He said the last statement with a self-satisfied sigh. They'd sent a clown in to kill me.

"You will never see again, and your life will be one of a sightless person." It wasn't what he'd said, it was how he'd said it.

Francois went on that morning, and then on and on and on, and since I couldn't reach him, I tried not to pay attention to him. But he laid open the inner wound again, and I lay bleeding as he jabbered. His reinstitution process was the instrument of evisceration. Francois perhaps did not even see the wound and ignored the bleeding. He kept on for some time before he congratulated me for not interrupting him and bid me *au revoir*.

Francois. *Saint Francois.* Saint of science and reinstitution. I made up my mind never to let him back in the room. I would listen carefully next time, measure my steps to the door and hit him as hard as I could before he could say anything. I was not a promising candidate for reinstitution.

As angry as I became over his intrusion, it also knocked me down, and I spiraled into a slippery downslope of depression after that. That afternoon, Sophie took one look at me and knew what had happened. She said little to me, but a few minutes later, I heard raised voices in the hallway. Sophie was confronting Dr. Bertrand, and he was getting the worse of it.

I did not see her again for two days, and I sank further down, refusing even to see Robert when he came to see me. Francois did not come again, I did not think he would, and neither did Dr. Bertrand. I demanded information from an orderly, but he would not say, and neither would the next one, even when I pleaded. The bandages remained on my head and over my eyes, and one night, angry and desperate, I roared like a bad, caged lion and ripped my bandages off. Two nurses I did not know raced in and my rage frightened them, so they called in three large male orderlies, who held me down while a nurse stabbed a needle into my arm. I heard one of them gasp before they put the new bandages back on my face. Then I slid into a misty place where a dark river ran through a grove of green oaks, and the dark form of the writer stood on the riverbank. He turned and looked at me and grinned and waved before I slid off into unconsciousness. *Nothing is what you think it is going to be.*

Chapter 31

During those weeks, Sophie continued to leave the hospital in the evenings out the side door. She always wore her hat and clearly did not want to be seen, yet she was followed one night. She went out the side door, kept to the shadows of the alley, despite the rats, and made the same turns on her way to the basement. She did not see the man in the trench coat, who was an experienced tracker, following her every move. She moved swiftly, but he easily kept up with her.

She hurried down the small French streets until she slowed as she came to the secret door. She used her key to open it quickly and slipped inside. The man in the trench coat moved fast, but the door was already shut by the time he reached it. He listened carefully with his ear to the door but couldn't hear anything.

Inside, Sophie walked down the stairs, followed the narrow hallway around a sharp corner, and walked farther under the bare lights that hung from the ceiling. She finally heard voices and knew the large basement room would be filled. She saw the guard at the door, and he waved to her. She walked inside and sighed. It always momentarily depressed her to come there, but she hid it entirely from the occupants. Around the edges of the room were tall, grim-looking men, many bearded and wearing hats. There was also a group of shorter men, who were darker and did not wear hats. All of them acknowledged Sophie as she entered the room. One man had a black dog at his side. A balding, bearded man walked quickly over to her and took her hat and coat.

"Hello," he said. "Thank you for coming. Without you, many of us would not know what to do. As you can see, there are many more tonight. They have begun to put out the word that you are here."

She nodded and put her hand on his shoulder.

"Just bring me one of your stories or sketches and I will be paid," she said.

He smiled and kissed her hand. "That I can do."

Then she took a deep breath and walked in among them all.

The next day, at the hospital, I received a surprise visit from Robert Meeshon and Inspector Jean-Claude. They shook hands in my room and Robert pulled out a small flask and handed it to me. I grinned and then winced as the powerful whiskey kicked down my throat.

"Ah, that's a fine thing, Robert," I said. I gripped the flask and took another drink.

"And it is illegal to have in a hospital," said the Inspector.

"Well," I said, "I can't see any police around."

They laughed.

"How are your eyes doing anyway?" Robert asked. I always appreciated his directness.

"The doctors reassure me that I'll never see again. They are a jolly bunch," I said. "There is someone here who I trust far more, and she tells me I am only in a temporary situation."

"Indeed," said Robert. "And is there anything more to tell about her?"

"Much more." I laughed. "But I'm not going to tell you. She's my beautiful secret weapon for right now."

Had I been able to see, I would have caught a curious and immediate look in the Inspector's eyes. He said nothing, though.

"Suit yourself man," Robert said with a laugh. "I'm bringing Allison next time, and she'll get it out of you."

"That's not fair, I am sure she will," I said.

"This is why so many in my business do not want women as inspectors," said Jean-Claude. "They undoubtedly would prove more effective than men, and soon we would all be out of our jobs."

We laughed.

A soft knocking came from the door and Jean-Claude opened it. Outside was one of his aides. He said something in a low voice to the Inspector, who turned to us. "It seems I am needed on another matter, I will be back. It won't be long."

We said quick goodbyes, then Robert sat down in one of the chairs. "I'm glad we are alone, Jake, I've wanted to talk to you."

"Oh, is this going to hurt?"

"Maybe."

"Shoot, then."

"I don't know any other way."

"Sure you do, you're one of the most tactful men I've ever met, but don't bother with preliminaries. We may not have time. What's on your mind?"

"Allison and I have talked about this several times. Usually because I'm guilty of what I want to talk about – although I think almost everyone is – at one time or another."

"Murder? Mayhem? Wanting to be able to see again?"

"Perfectionism, Jake. It's something we all don't talk about enough, but it can be murder and mayhem and it sure as hell keeps us from seeing ourselves properly much of the time."

I was silent. Robert was being uncharacteristically clumsy. "Oh?" was all I said.

"People think being obsessed with being perfect is a good thing. To be driven by perfectionism can make people feel self-righteous. But, most often, it's a snake that gets you in its coils. It starts squeezing subtly and you can't even feel it until it starts breaking your bones."

I turned my head in his direction. I still wasn't sure where this was going.

"Some of the most accomplished people in the world are driven by it."

"What's wrong with that?"

"Ah, but that's the point," said Robert. "People see great artists accomplish great things and they believe it's because these artists are perfectionists. So, from the outside, it looks like a good thing. People want to be like them and then they begin to brag about being perfectionists and they infect their children with it. But, it is not a good thing, Jake. It's a bad thing. Believing you have to be perfect all the time will sink you like a stone. It can kill you if you don't get past it."

I frowned. Was he talking about me? Why else would

he have brought this up?

"You think I am a perfectionist?"

"What do you think?" he said. "But ultimately, that's up to you to decide." "We all are, at some point and just because you get past holding yourself to an impossible standard of perfection once, doesn't mean you won't pin yourself up against it some other time on some other issue. It's when you do it to yourself all the time that it becomes dangerous, even lethal. You can't win that battle. It will kill you."

"What the hell are you talking about, Robert? Are you patronizing me?"

"No. You know I'm not. Look, there is an artist here in Paris who paints water lilies. You know him. He is a perfectionist. What's important to know is that he is not a great artist because of that, he is a great artist because of his soul and his drive for excellence. Excellence, Jake. Not perfectionism. His perfectionism is killing him. He tore up fifteen of his greatest paintings a few years ago because he didn't think they were perfect. He thinks he is a failure. He's successful, rich, adored, and miserable."

"How do you know he would have been any good if he wasn't a perfectionist?"

"Part of this is semantics, Jake. I'm not saying trying to be perfect is a problem, I'm saying that believing you have to be perfect all the time is. The fact is, the more mistakes you make and the more you admit and learn from them, the better you're going to be at what you do – including writing and relationships."

"It sounds too easy."

"It's not."

"I don't trust it."

"Promise to think a little about it."

"Robert, it doesn't sound manly."

"Oh for Christ's sake, Jake.

Just then, the door opened and Jean-Claude came in. I was relieved. The conversation with Robert had things churning inside me.

"Jake, I have a question for you," Jean-Claude said.

I waited.

"As you know, we are still searching for the band of thieves, mostly gypsies I suppose, one of whom attacked you," he said. "We have reason to believe they meet in an underground room, a basement of sorts, near here. There is some intelligence that they have banded with the Communists, for what reason we do not know. We've had the area under surveillance for the past few days. One of our men has seen a young, attractive woman, wearing a man's hat, leaving this hospital every other night. She walks the back alleys down to the basement. He tried to follow her inside, but the door was locked when he got there, and she did not leave by the same door."

"In other words, this amateur gave your man the slip." I laughed, but I was hoping to hide the fear I felt inside. "Like we said, women are better at this."

Jean-Claude chuckled but stayed on the topic.

"This could be a big break for us, Jake. She might even be the leader of this gang of cutthroats. If you hear of anyone coming and going like that – a woman in a hat, probably a nurse – please let me know right away. We would like to ultimately find the man who put you in here."

"Thank you, Inspector. I would like to find him myself. This has been a complete nightmare. Is there anything else about this woman I should know?"

Jean-Claude was silent for a moment. Then he said, "Yes, she has dark hair, black even, and from her stealth, it is apparent she knows she is doing something against the law." He hesitated. I was sure he was watching to see if I had a reaction to that. Luckily, my eyes couldn't give me away.

"I see," I said. "I'll be on the lookout for a beautiful, dark-haired, woman wearing a hat, who is smarter than we are and who likes Communists and gypsies."

"That would about cover it," said Jean-Claude, and I thought I caught a hint of displeasure in his voice.

"I'm sorry, Inspector. I don't mean to make light of it. I want these bastards as much as you do, and I appreciate everything you are doing more than you could know. If I hear anything, I will let you know immediately."

Robert came over and gave me a hug.

"We'll find them, Jake. You worry about getting better and put your money on your beautiful secret weapon. Doctors are far overrated."

Jean-Claude put his hand on my shoulder. "I am sure you know what you are doing Jake. I trust you will make the right decision. I also want you to get well as soon as possible. There is much more illegal whiskey to drink."

We laughed, and they left. Then I sat down heavily on the bed, stunned and scared. Later, I would think more about what Robert and I had discussed, but right then I was focused on Jean-Claude's suspicions.

What was Sophie up to?

I knew about her mysterious disappearances from the hospital. The orderlies, doctors and nurses gossiped, and I had become an excellent eavesdropper. I tried to put it out of my mind because of one terrifying possibility I had wanted to hide from myself. She had a gypsy lover.

What I'd heard from the Inspector all but confirmed it. I suddenly hated Apollinaire with a white-hot passion. I hated that Sophie and I had talked about his damn poem about a gypsy lover. Had Sophie been laughing at me the entire time? The thought nearly broke me in half. I groaned and doubled over. Then I thought about Sophie and saw her face clearly in my mind, and I knew she was not capable of laughing at me, but I wasn't sure of the other. Maybe she'd known this other man from before me. Maybe she wanted to protect me from how she felt about him. But then why sneak off like a thief in the night? Was he a wanted man? My mind raced into a million corners, none of which offered shelter to me and none of which seemed real.

After a time, I lay back in the bed and finished off the flask Robert had left with me. The whiskey burned again going down, and it felt comforting. I was having no luck in trying to control my thoughts or emotions. They flew wild and dangerous, like big debris in a hurricane. At one point, I thought of Apollinaire's stupid poems about gypsies, and then I remembered how one ended:

> We knew quite well that we were damned
> But, hope of love in the street
> Made us think hand in hand
> Of what the Gypsy did foresee

That suddenly didn't seem so bad to me. I didn't care much for the "love in the street" part, but I liked that whatever relationship they had was "damned," or at least that was how I chose to interpret the line. Still, I was miserable. I couldn't see my way out of it, and then I laughed bitterly. "See my way out of it!" It was a dark joke and I didn't laugh long.

Just before midnight, I heard Sophie softly open the door to my room. My whole body was electrified with fear, pain, anger, worry and concern and it all jumped out of my chest and into my head at once and I lay mute, but breathing hard.

"I know you heard me," she whispered.

"Yes," I said. "I heard you, and others saw you, too."

"What?"

"You've been spotted. The police think your lover's rendezvous is part of a plot to help some Communists and gypsies. I didn't tell them you are only helping one damn gypsy."

"Jake! What are you talking about?"

"Your lover, Sophie! I know all about the son of a bitch!"

"No, Jake, what about the police?"

"Oh, so that's it. The other doesn't matter, just the police."

"Jake!" She came over to the bed, and I could feel the heat from her even before she grabbed my arms and shook me hard.

"What are you talking about? Tell me! Tell me and shut up about any lover. Just tell me about the police! This is really important. What do you know?"

"I know enough," I said, trying to be contemptuous, but it came out badly.

"Did the police come here?"

Suddenly, I realized there was more happening than I knew. Sophie might really have been in trouble. I sat up.

"My friend Inspector Jean-Claude came over with Robert," I said slowly. "They were pretending it was just a social visit, but Jean-Claude was after something – someone – and I think that someone was you."

I told her what the Inspector had told me, including her description and the fact that she was being followed.

She gasped.

"Sophie, I know there is something else, and I want to hear about it and help you, but please, first tell me – have you been seeing a gypsy lover?"

She let out an exasperated breath. "Yes Jake, I have, and I do love them, all twenty of them. But none of them are more than eight years old

"What?"

"I have been providing medical care for the children of some people who can't go to the hospitals or they will be arrested. Many of these children are malnourished and sick. That's where I go. Jake, I'm sorry to have to say this, but you are an idiot too. I have no lover."

"My God," I said.

"Yes, and you are lucky that both of us have so much patience with you."

"These are mainly thieves and Communists you're seeing?"

"No, I am seeing the children, who are neither thieves nor Communists nor anything else. They are just children until we make them into something else. I only deal with one man, who seems to be the leader. I think he is one of them, but he is a writer and painter, and a very nice man."

"An artist. What does he look like?"

"I don't know," she said impatiently. "Like the others, tall, balding, has a beard. He has a Spanish name, but he is an American."

"Dos Passos." I said. "He would do that for children."

"Yes, I heard him called that."

"Ah, then we have to protect him – and them – from the police. Tomorrow morning, early Sophie, you must go there but without your hat and without going down the alleyways. The police will never suspect you walking down the main boulevards. You must tell them the place has been made by the authorities and they must move quickly, before lunchtime."

Sophie put her hand on my arm. "I will."

"And, Sophie, if any of the children are in real danger because of their sickness, bring them here, and I will say they are my kin."

She didn't say anything for a long moment. "You have just rescued yourself as well, Jake. I was angry that you thought I had a secret lover, but you are forgiven for that now."

She leaned over and kissed my lips.

"Sweet idiot," she murmured.

I kissed her back, and we held each other for a long time. After she left, I wanted to shout, and then I laughed out loud. There was no lover! The heavens were indeed being patient with me, and luckily, so was she.

Chapter 32

In the morning, Sophie left early, and she did not come back until just before lunch time. There was a commotion at my door, and then it banged open and I knew it was Dr. Bertrand because he was talking imperiously to Sophie and somebody else.

"See here, this is highly unusual!" he said, in an irritated voice. "This is a hospital for certain types, and I don't know if we can just be taking in children from the streets because of the say-so of Ms. Masson and this…this….gentleman." Bertrand was stuttering. I could tell he was angry, and I wondered how much this would cost Sophie professionally.

No one had prepared me, and I had no idea whom Sophie had brought back to the hospital.

"Dr. Bertrand," I said with as much authority as I could. "All I can say is I trusted your staff and your own substantial generosity to take in these…"

"Nephews," Sophie said quickly.

"Nephews of mine for the short time it will take these young souls and bodies to heal. I will pay double the cost, and I will put in a good word for you with my good friend, the Police Inspector."

I whispered the next part.

"I know they suspect there is a spy in this hospital who is helping the Communists. They are watching this place, you know. It won't hurt to reassure them that the hospital administration is doing everything it can to catch this spy."

I could hear Dr. Bertrand shuffle his feet for a second.

"All right then," he said, still not happy. "We will take your *nephews* in, but only until they are well enough to be moved to their homes, wherever they are. Not one day longer."

He slammed the door on his way out.

I heard Sophie and Passos laugh quietly.

"Well done, monsieur," the man said to me. "I am John Dos Passos. I am very pleased to meet you and to thank you for everything you have done."

He leaned down and gave me a bear hug.

"You have quite a family, I might add," he said, and I could tell he was smiling. "One of your nephews is quite blond with blue eyes and the other is every bit as dark, with eyes the color of shiny coal."

"All the better." I laughed. "I want to give Dr. Bertrand as much indigestion as possible. That should do it."

"I would ask why a stranger would stick his neck out for us, when he has nothing in the game," he said. "Now that I know what, or should I say 'whom', you have in the game, I understand. If life is not about that, it is not about anything."

He stood and I knew he was hugging Sophie. They spoke to each other, and he promised to be back in touch when they found a new and safer place. We had no way of knowing what would happen to him. We just knew that at that moment, the room was full of warmth and respect.

He left, and then Sophie left to help the children get settled into their small room where the nurses doted on them in the days to come.

Chapter 33

Two days later, I was awakened early in the morning. I thought I was still dreaming, when I heard Sophie. I reached out to her in my dream, and she took my hand. She squeezed it tightly, and I quickly realized it was not a dream; she was standing next to my bed. Suddenly, her lips were by my ear.

"Shh, no one knows I'm here," she whispered. "I was nearly suspended from the hospital for arguing with Dr. Bertrand, but they are stubborn like goats, and they are as wrong as goats. Is that English, 'wrong as goats'?" She didn't wait for me to answer. "I have seen more eye injuries than they have. They *are* wrong as goats." This time she laughed a little. Then she lay down next to me on top of the covers, and gently slipped her arm under my neck. Instantly, I was awake – all of me, I noticed.

"I have been thinking," she said. "In a few days, they are going to let you leave here. I was planning to visit Flers, my old village then, and I'd like you to come with me."

"Why would you?"

"I think it would be good."

"I couldn't see it."

"You see a lot of things."

"Not a town."

"Maybe not, but I need you. This won't be easy for me."

"Especially with a blind man stumbling about. You can't want that."

"Jake! I have thought this through. I want you to come. For me."

I was thrilled and frightened. I tried to hide the latter part.

I realized then that I didn't want to face the world without her. She knew that already, though.

"You are offering me charity," I said.

"I knew you would say that. So, you want me to sock you again?"

"No."

"Then please do not say that. We are past that. Don't make me sock you."

"Okay."

"We have to take a train. It will be about twenty-four hours because there are many delays. I haven't been back since a few months after the war."

It was quiet for a moment and she shivered against me.

"I will be scared."

"Don't be."

"Yes, I will be. That is why I want you there."

"What can I possibly do? I can't see anything."

"Yes, you can Jake. You see me."

"Yes," I said.

Right then, I admitted to myself what I had known for some time. I was in love with her. When I knew that, I knew I had never been in love with Margaret or anyone else because it had not been like this. Nothing had ever been like this. This was somehow fast and slow at the same time, desperate and calm, and I felt old and brand new. I knew I was in love, and that was all I knew right then.

I told her, "Okay then, we'll go on the train. Just don't let me fall off."

She balled her fist and put it playfully into my ribs. "No," she said. "I will not let you fall off. You will not get away from me that easily."

There are times, tones, words, and moments you will always recall no matter what else happens to you in your life or in that relationship afterward. It's easy to think of them. You remember exactly how you felt, what it smelled like, and what you saw, and sometimes, especially when you are empty and alone, you want to feel that way again. But you're mostly glad you got to feel that way even once.

I felt that way when I touched her face and realized her eyes were shut, and I touched them until I bent over and kissed them, too. She did not resist, so I kissed her cheek and then moved down and put my lips on her lips. She kissed back for a long time. I held her tightly and she seemed to tremble for a moment, and then she shifted and held me tighter. I traced her neck with my fingers and felt what love felt like, and then I put my hand under her hair, which was a waterfall of silk. Then I found I was hard, and she stirred, and our lips gently explored each other's, and lingered and hung there. I was happy that I was a man and that she was a witch doctor, a shaman, a magic woman.

Then an orderly banged on the door and came in backward. They always did that. They held their trays full of food and came in backward. He dropped something onto the floor, with a clang. Sophie was up and off the bed in a flash.

"What's this?" she said sharply.

"I'm sorry, mademoiselle. I was bringing an early breakfast. I am sorry, I did not mean to intrude."

"There was nothing to intrude upon! You are too early to bring breakfast. Go out and come back in an hour," she said.

The orderly left quickly.

Sophie came back over to the bed, but did not get back in. She kissed me again, though. We held it, and then she pulled back.

We didn't say anything for a moment. Then I found her hand with mine. "Thank you," I said. I was going to say more, but she held her fingers to my lips.

"I have to go," she said. "I will buy the orderly a bottle of Bordeaux and he won't say anything. You will go on the train with me then?"

"Yes," I said. "No matter where the train goes."

Chapter 34

Three days later, my hospital stay was over. The doctor took the big bandages off and left a small dressing on my forehead and gauze strips around my eyes. He was as brusque as ever. In the end, he curtly wished me luck and told me not to trust anyone who was not a science man or a man of medicine. He had to attend to other patients. He left, and I heard his hard footsteps all the way down the hall until he turned the corner and was gone.

Earlier, Sophie had instructed the orderly not to touch my things. He was polite to me, and I suspected he might have gotten two bottles of Bordeaux. She packed my things herself. Robert and Allison had come by the day before, and we had talked quietly in the garden, which was in a small open square inside the hospital. I had been able to smell flowers planted on either side of us, although what kind they were, I did not know.

"Margaret has left Paris," Robert told me. I was not surprised.

"With the painter?" I'd asked.

"No, she went back to New York by herself, although we heard she has a musician there who is quite mad for her," Allison said.

"Did she say anything about me?"

"No, but I am certain she was worried about you," Robert said.

"Robert! Margaret worries about Margaret," Allison said.

Robert laughed.

"She was beautiful," I said.

"She is a survivor," said Allison.

"She had to be," Robert added. "And you, Jake, will survive too. But you must find a way to start writing again."

In my mind, I'd bid a final and peaceful goodbye to Margaret – and to that part of my life – and then slowly allowed Robert's compliment to fire me up inside. I could have collapsed; he was betting I wouldn't.

When they left, they made me promise to stay with them after Sophie and I returned. I promised, and we hugged before they left.

Sophie finished packing my things, and we left the hospital at ten o'clock in the morning. She had a cab waiting, and we rode to the train station and boarded before mid-day. She held my hand as we walked and whispered to me what was coming, so I knew where to put my feet. I walked very slowly and once in a while, stumbled, and often the loud, sharp sounds of the street and everyday life startled me. That part was hard. I kept taking deep breaths, and I could not allow myself to think about doing it that way the rest of my life. People with sight challenges did, of course, and they lived lives as full or fuller than others, but I didn't think I had the courage to do that, not yet anyway.

Courage had become a key word for me. I told Robert later that it was a damn inadequate word, wretchedly short of properly giving weight to this thing – this courage. As Sophie walked me through the streets, I thought about that. I wondered where courage came from. Genetics? Is that why some have it and some don't? Why some seem to have a majestic amount of it and others just a little, and yet others earn it or gain it as they go along, and suddenly one day, when they need it, it's there, depthless, powerful, and huge?

Sophie seemed happy, if pensive, when we settled in and the train began to move. I knew she was concerned about going back. I felt about as useful to her as a piece of luggage, but she reached for my hand and squeezed it, which made me happy and elevated above luggage.

On the train, I could smell coffee, tobacco, leather, and Sophie's intoxicating perfume, which was my favorite. Sophie was quiet, no doubt watching the last vestiges of Paris rumble by. I saw blackness and heard some chattering voices around us in the train car, but mostly, I felt the hard rhythm of the big iron wheels, which rattled over the small spaces left open where the rail lengths met.

Later that night, after Sophie went to sleep, I thought more about it. Lying near her, I thought about how women who had true courage were the most appealing and worthwhile of all women. Often people don't see their courage because they don't flaunt it. Nations don't erect statues of courageous women and mothers like they do captains of industry, generals, or presidents. But a man lucky enough to find a woman with true courage must never lose her. That would be the biggest tragedy of his life.

It was some time before Sophie spoke. I sensed that most of the people had left our car to go up the rolling corridor to the dining cars, which were three cars up, toward the engine.

"Jake, I need to tell you something."

"Oh. Is it good?"

"I think so, but I'm not sure how you will take it."

"Hmm. That doesn't sound good."

"We have met before," she said.

I didn't understand.

"We have met before – you and me. On a street. In Paris."

"Is this about reincarnation? Because if it is, I have a great one to tell you about how I was once the prince of Persia."

"I'm serious, Jake. We met once before you came to the hospital."

"What are you talking about?"

"Yes," she said in a low voice. "I had my arms full of bags and you were sweet. You asked if I were a nurse, but you didn't ask my name. Remember?"

I thought back, and then I was stunned. I had seen Sophie before! I knew what she looked like in my mind. Suddenly, all was chaos in my brain. I had painstakingly constructed an image of her face in my mind in the past few weeks, building it through my fingers by touching her face, brow, nose, cheeks, chin and lips. I loved her face, she was extraordinarily beautiful to me. Now, that image collided mightily with the other visual image from our meeting on the street. They were like two ships ramming at sea. My head spun, and the two images fought and blended and fought again until the two separated, and I thought all I could remember was the image of her on the street. Then that faded, and the other came in. Then, in one splendid moment, the two images came together and made one beautiful picture of Sophie, and I could find no seam in it. It was a feeling of completeness I had never had in my life before.

"Okay," I said finally. "That is you. But why did you wait so long to tell me?"

"I don't know. I liked how you went about exploring my face with your hands and I didn't want to ruin it."

"You wouldn't have."

"I wouldn't?"

"No."

"I'm glad. I worried a little."

"I think I fell for you a little bit on the sidewalk that day. Now I'm glad it was you. Otherwise, there would have been a problem."

She laughed.

"I did ask you if I could be of service, didn't I? Lord. That was the worst for me."

She laughed again. "Well, thank you for offering."

"I wish you wouldn't have remembered that."

"You were dazzled."

"Yes, that's surely it. Otherwise, I would have been perfect."

A silence fell. I could sense Sophie was thinking and had something to tell me she thought was important. I was not wrong.

"There is no perfect in art and love, Jake," she said softly.

I sat back. I thought about that for a long time. I still think about it. I heard my dad roaring in the clouds over that remark, and the war then would begin, and he would look like Zeus, mad and full of fire and rain. Just then, the train hit a rough connection on the rails and swung violently for a moment, spilling our coffee. I felt it hot and steaming on my knees. Sophie made a sound of dismay, and we were busied with cleaning up after.

That night, Zeus appeared again in my dreams, scowling at me, and I fell under a hammer of judgment. Then a goat appeared, and turned toward me and it had Margaret's face, and then the goat's body changed into Margaret's body. Her eyes met mine, and I saw pain there, and I nodded slightly to her, and then she swept upward and over a mountain and was gone. Sophie and I were suddenly together on the street, where I watched her and touched her face, and she turned in slow motion and smiled at me as if we had been happy together for a long time. It was a strange dream, and I tried not to think about it afterward, except for the last part.

The next morning was a passing of small villages, horses, and farm wagons. Sophie described the brown and green fields stretching out away from the train to the low hills beyond. Some had not yet recovered from the war. Sometimes she would tell me about a farmhouse she saw that was no more than a blackened hull, faded now with the rain. The rugged walls often led abruptly to craters where the shells had hit. I knew the sight brought back memories for her, and she shrank back a little from time to time, and her voice had a tremor more than once, but she did not talk about it or make any kind of scene. It would have been okay with me if she had, but I knew she had to deal with this in her own way.

That night, we reached Flers and rode in an old English army jeep that now served as the village taxi to a small hotel on the other end of the town. It wasn't much of a hotel. It had come to life nearly two hundred years before as a grand

barn on a nobleman's estate. The estate had not withstood
the philandering of the grandchildren and had fallen into
disrepair. It was finally sold and used, for a while, to shelter
horses and wagons. It had served several wars until, near the
turn of the century, it was turned into a place for overnight
travelers.

There were four rooms, and they were all empty. Sophie
picked the best one, which had a bed and a couch. The
bathroom was at the end of the hallway, but since we were
the only ones there, we had it to ourselves. She quickly
unpacked our clothes, and we sat downstairs by a little
fireplace, sipping wine and eating small croissants the hotel
owner's wife had made for us. Sophie did not talk much, and
that was okay with me.

It was quiet and relaxing after the long train ride. When
the wine and bread were gone, we said goodnight to the
hotel owner's wife. She was sweet and had a nice voice, and
she made wonderful croissants. Sophie took my arm and we
went upstairs.

I wondered what the sleeping arrangements would be. I
also wondered if she expected me to try to win my way into
bed with her. If it was done with sufficient tact and respect,
most women would forgive a man an advance if she was not
ready for it, but few would forgive a man for not advancing
if she was ready for it. But the blindness took all that out
of me, and I found myself shy and reluctant to try anything
at all. Not that making love to Sophie hadn't crossed my
mind but making a pass at her seemed silly right then, out of
rhythm and not worthy of us.

Without discussing it, I heard Sophie making up the
couch for me. We held hands for a moment at the door to
the bedroom, and I felt her hand on the back of my neck.

I leaned forward, and our lips met. It was disconcerting for me to lean forward like that and not be sure of what would happen. If she hadn't been there, I would have just sailed through the air and crashed face-first into the furniture. I trusted her though, and she was there. She didn't guide my lips to hers as much as she placed them in my way. I could sense everything about her then, her scent, the satin of her skin, and silk of her hair, and how it flowed down around my cheek. Somehow, I knew her eyes were shut, and so we kissed from the inside out, and then from the outside back in, and that is the way it feels when you are blind. I thought we would spend the whole night holding each other and never sleep, and even when I expected her to retire from me, she did not. Finally, we broke off, and she shivered. She put her face into my chest. I knew it wasn't just one thing. It was us mingled with the grief she had for her village and for her parents and maybe something else. I was glad to be there for her, and I held her for a long time until she finally sighed and left me and went to bed. I was awake a long time after.

Chapter 35

The following morning was a Sunday, and Sophie insisted we go to the chapel. There was a service, and we sang a hymn and sat together. Sophie quietly described the inside of the church for me, and after a while, she mentioned that an old man, in long, ancient trousers, probably the best pair he owned, she thought, was sitting across from us, and he kept looking at us. I didn't think much of it and afterward, Sophie called the taxi. She wanted to see the rest of the town and finally go out to the ruins of her home and the farm where she had been raised.

She talked quietly and constantly while we drove through the village. It was not what she remembered. She knew it as it had been for centuries before the war, but the shells from three different armies had burst it all into the ground, and a new kind of town had emerged, one built almost entirely of new wood, mortar and plaster. It was not modern or fancy, but it was new. Little of the old remained.

"I am a stranger here," she said. "I know none of this."

"Maybe that is good," I said.

"It doesn't feel good."

"I am sorry."

"There was nothing left after the bombs."

"Now there is."

"Yes, but maybe people don't care what happened anymore."

"Of course, they do. They care. They are just trying to find a new way to keep living."

"Is that what I'm doing, Jake? Am I just trying to find a new way to keep living? That is so sad."

"No," I said. "We all do that. It is not sad, only at first."

"What I knew isn't here anymore."

"But what you know now is." I kissed her. It was a clumsy kiss that landed somewhere on her ear, but it made her laugh.

Still, she was quiet for a time after that. We drove out of the village onto a long dirt road. It led between long, wavy rows of wine grapes, and Sophie told me they had replaced the barley fields that had been there before the war. The bombs and the armies had destroyed nearly everything and blown huge holes in the fields. The fields had been leveled after the war and now the young wine grapes grew, and there were a few blossoms, but that didn't seem to calm Sophie. Her anxiety grew as we drew closer to her old home. We drove up a rise and then back down, when she gasped and uttered a terrible little cry of pain that drew back across the ages of all mothers and daughters who had suffered in wars – wars they never started, but in which they always suffered. An icy shiver ran down my spine, and I heard the taxi driver shift in his seat.

"You must tell me what you see," I said.

"I…I cannot."

"You must. Otherwise it won't come out. You won't be rid of it."

"It is burned. It is gone. The barn, the house, the little summer cottage where I played every day. It's only rubble there now. It is all gone."

Her voice was thin. I touched her fingers.

The cab stopped. I asked the driver to come back for us in two hours. He gratefully drove off and we were left alone.

We walked to the place where her childhood home had once stood.

"There is nothing much here," she said, her voice wavering.

"Tell me how it used to be."

She didn't say anything at first, but then she began talking, and I could tell she was leading me to where each room had stood.

"The kitchen was here, and my parents' room was over there."

She remained composed until she got to the living room, where her father's chair and the fireplace had been, where he'd read her books and told her stories. Then she sat heavily on the ground and began to cry.

I sat next to her and didn't say anything.

She cried quietly for a long time. I held her for a while, and then I stood and walked slowly around, feeling things with my feet and hands. I found the old fireplace. The river rock was still there in a rubbled pile, and I could almost feel the love they had shared in front of the fire. Sophie stopped crying and I sensed she was watching me feel my way around

"Our lives were so different," she said. "Our fathers were different."

"This is where your father read you books about horses," I said.

"Yes."

"I can hear his voice," I said.

"And my mother's."

"Yes."

"Can you see them?"

"Yes, they loved you."

"I need for you to see them, too."

"I do."

The wind blew a little then and the air felt good on our faces.

Sophie stopped crying. We sat without speaking for a time. I do not know what I was thinking when the bright light blew up in my face. I suddenly saw white and silver explosions, and instantly I feared the bombs were back, and I grabbed Sophie and pulled her to the ground. We lay there for a long moment before Sophie gently pushed me off her. Oddly, there was no noise. There had been no explosion. There was only the rustle of a new wind.

"What are you doing?" Sophie asked softly, stroking my face. "What is happening?"

"I…I saw a flashing light. I saw it flash. It went off in my head. I thought it was a bomb."

"What? Jake, what? You saw a light?"

Just then, another light, smaller and softer but quick and jagged like lightning, went off in my head. I flinched and ducked.

"There! There it is again! Did you see it?"

"No, Jake. There is no light. You are seeing lights?"

"Two. I only saw two."

"It's happening! It's happening then! Oh, Jake!"

"What? What is happening?" I was confused. Sophie sounded excited.

"The Polish village!" Her laughter came out in a joyous and excited burst. "That is what happened. It's happening in your eyes."

I suddenly got excited, even though I didn't quite know what she was saying.

"Do you remember our conversation? I never believed your eyes were permanently damaged. I told you the doctors were wrong. These bright flashes are part of it. It will take time, but you are going to see again, Jake. Those lights are the first sign!"

I sat, stunned. I was afraid to believe her, but I had seen the lights. I would not have believed anything, though, if not for her.

Suddenly, she grabbed my hand and squeezed it hard.

"Jake, someone is coming."

"Who?"

"I do not know. I just heard footsteps on the other side of the wall."

Then I heard them too and jumped to my feet in pure instinct. I was a fighter, and I had no fear of who was coming, except now I couldn't see them. It occurred to me once I stood up that I wasn't going to be able to do much good fighting, but then Sophie let out a sigh of relief.

"It is the old man from the church this morning," she said.

I could hear his shuffling footsteps as he came out from behind the broken chimney.

"*Bonsoir*," he said.

"*Bonsoir*," said Sophie. "Who are you?" She spoke in English, for my benefit.

"I am Ernesto," he answered. I sensed from his hesitant, soft voice that he probably meant us no harm. Still, I was cautious.

"Why are you here?" I asked.

"Excuse me, I did not mean to intrude or alarm you," he said. "It's just that I thought I recognized you, mademoiselle, at the church. I knew you when you grew up here. I am Ernesto, your father's friend."

Sophie cried out and stepped over to embrace the old man.

"Ernesto! Oh, oh, oh," she said joyfully, hugging him.

I heard him choke back a cry, and then I heard sobs from him.

"I did not recognize you. I did not think anyone was left. I did not know. I am sorry, but I am so happy to see you."

She brought him over to me. "Jake, this is Ernesto. He would often come for dinner. And he is here now! This is a miracle!"

The older man must have been pleased because he couldn't say anything for a moment.

"I would not be here if not for you," he said to Sophie, finally. Then he turned to me. "She saved many people during the worst of it. She was everywhere and she had no fear. People were dying, and most did die, but some didn't, and most who didn't were touched by her, monsieur. She was an angel from heaven. I have come to thank her. *Mon agne.*"

"Get up, Ernesto!" she said, and I knew she felt wonderful that the old man had come. "You do not need to kiss my hand. I should kiss yours. I did what I could do, nothing more. Now! Let us talk about how you have been, and then the days before."

They spent the rest of the morning talking nearly non-stop in French as I walked through the ruins of the house, feeling the stones with my hands. I saw no more flashes, but I wondered if Sophie could be right. I worked hard to strike a balance in my brain – some hope and some practicality. I thought of how I would learn to write again with no sight. But I also allowed myself to imagine what it would be like to see Paris again and, of course, Sophie.

After a time, she broke out the lunch she had made for us, baguettes, cheese, and some fine ham. We shared it with him, and we drank a bottle of wine together. He and Sophie laughed much and cried together too.

At one point, Ernesto gave in to his curiosity about the bandages on my eyes. "Does it hurt?" he asked.

I laughed. "No, but it makes it hard to see."

He laughed a little, relieved that his question hadn't offended me. "I was walking by the river in Paris," I said. "I had a fight with a man who tried to steal from me."

"I hope you ferociously pummeled him," Ernesto said in French, and Sophie translated for me.

"No, but I wish I would have. He was quick, but after he hit me, he called for help to bring me to the hospital. He was a strange kind of thief."

"Yes," said the older man thoughtfully. "That is a strange thief. Perhaps he did not mean to hit you."

"No, he meant to hit me, and he hit me hard. He was scared. I meant to hit him hard too, but I missed."

"Well, he is a son of a bitch then. Someday he might end up in the river."

I smiled. "He was small. A fish would eat him."

"And that would serve him right!" exclaimed Ernesto and we laughed, although talking about the thief stirred up some anger in me. I tried not to show it.

As the time for the taxi approached, Ernesto asked where Sophie's parents were buried. He had been trying to protect his own family during that time and did not know what had happened to them.

"The bombs," Sophie said simply. "They blew everything up. They are with the stars now. The night sky is the only monument I have for them."

The older man was quiet for a moment. Then he jumped to his feet and exclaimed, "We must make something for them here then!"

I liked the idea immediately. "Help me!" I said.

Among the three of us, we had enough strength to lift a large, flat stone from the fireplace Sophie and I had been sitting on and carry it down a little hill to a beautiful green bank of the small clear creek. Sophie's family had relied on the creek for clean water for nearly more than a century. We dug a foundation for it in the soft soil and anchored it, so it was level and solid. Even the high water in springtime would not wash the stone away.

"Later, I will come back here and chisel their beloved names in this stone," promised Ernesto.

"Yes, it will be here forever," I said. "We will come back to see you and come here and drink wine and share more stories, and they will remain alive in our hearts." It sounded a bit formal when I said it, but somehow it seemed appropriate, and Sophie was pleased.

"Yes!" she said. "We will come back often together, and it will always be good to remember the good things."

"*Oui!*" exclaimed Ernesto. "That we will do!"

The taxi came later, and we hugged the older man, and he and Sophie cried. We promised again to return, climbed in and the taxi slowly left and climbed the hill. We had gone only a short distance, when Sophie suddenly asked the cab driver to stop. She did not get out, and she did not say anything, but I could tell she was looking at something.

"What is it?" I asked.

She said nothing for a time, and the taxi driver and I waited patiently. Finally, she took my arm and slowly told me the story of the English soldier and the bombing that had gone on for four days and nights.

"We did not believe we would live through it," she said softly. "I was seventeen years old. I don't think I loved him, but it was as if we were the only two people left in the world. The war did not let him live long after we came out, but he lived then, during those four days and nights."

I realized she was asking for my understanding. "Of course," I said. "If I had a glass of our wine, I would toast to him. I would toast to the English soldier and to you and then to us."

She cried for just a moment and then kissed me. I knew instinctively that would be nearly all the crying there was because when you got something in the right place, there was sadness perhaps and some appreciation, but the grief was eased, and that was when you knew you could trust, and love could be good again. She leaned against me on the ride back to the hotel.

It was dark by the time we got back to our little hotel, and we washed our faces and hands and went downstairs and down the street to the only restaurant in town. We shared a fine dinner that included a deep green salad with goat cheese, tomatoes, figs, and sugared almonds. We also had a bottle of white wine from the Loire Valley.

We paid the bill and walked slowly back the hotel. Sophie told me the moon was out, and I thought I could feel it on my arms. She kissed me and then playfully pretended it hadn't been her kissing me but the mischievous moon.

"It is trying to stir up trouble," she said.

"It was a wonderful kiss," I said. "If that is the case, then I am in love with this French moon."

"Love, monsieur?" Sophie asked, her voice warm, teasing and electric.

"Yes." There was no tease in my voice. "Because it is true. I love you, Sophie."

"Jake....oh!....Oh!...Are you sure? It isn't just...."

"That I am blind and mixing up love with being thankful to you for taking care of me?"

"Yes, that's exactly what I fear," she said.

"Please don't fear that," I said. "I thought of that a long time ago. It's simple. I love you with everything a man's got. You have courage and you are beautiful, and Ernesto is right. You are an angel. I love you, and that's it."

"And that's it," Sophie said softly. "Oh, how I wish I could see your eyes."

"You would find them too gone for you, and you would laugh, but you would see they are as true and as wild for you as the rest of me."

She moved inside my arms and kissed me.

"I guess it is what you Americans call official then," she said. "We are in love. We love each other because I love you with everything a woman's got."

"You love me?"

"Yes, I very much love you, and I have for some time. I think since you were such an idiot about the gypsy." She giggled. "And maybe before, even. So, it is official."

So it was that a blind, struggling American writer and a beautiful witchdoctor who practiced her craft under the crowned and golden lights of Paris, found each other and laughed and held each other under a promiscuous French moon. We could not have let go of each other if we'd tried, and neither of us tried until we were back in our room. That was when I finally could not stand it any longer and began to unbutton her blouse. She laughed sweetly and let me do it.

I ran my hands under her blouse and over her breasts, which provided the most divine sense of softness and life I had ever felt. It was so intense I lost my focus and fumbled the last two buttons.

She didn't move and let me start over.

"Thank you for trusting me," I said.

"I love you, and we do not need to talk about trust," she said, slipping into the cool sheets. She gasped slightly as I slid in next to her, and the electric current of our two bodies touching shot through us and into the night sky all the way to the mischievous moon. "I feel trust in your heart," she said, holding her hand to my chest.

"Yes," I said. "And lust everywhere else."

"Yes." She laughed. "I can feel that too."

She started to murmur something but stopped and gasped as I stroked and kissed her neck and then her firm, smooth breasts again. There was a slow and barely controlled urgency to my caresses. It was the freest, most pleasurable and instinctive thing I'd ever done. I touched her neck with the backs of my fingers and slid them down over her shoulders and finally kissed her breasts, teasing them gently. They felt to me like rose petals, and it was astounding to receive all those incredibly erotic points of love through senses other than my eyes.

Her chest rose up, she moved her thighs, and her hair slipped across the pillow, and then she rolled on top of me and kissed me hard. I was more aroused than I had ever been; there was no army that could have kept me from making love with Sophie that night.

I held her tightly, and she let her body lie flat against mine.

"I love you," she murmured, and I kissed her and said it back many times.

We were not shy with each other. She touched me

slowly at first, then with some energy, and then almost frantically. She touched my face, shoulders, arms, and chest, then slid her hands to my thighs and, finally to the center, where I was trying to reach the moon. She grasped me and murmured something in French. I didn't know what it was, but I liked the sound of it. She pulled me slightly, wanting me on top of her.

But the moon was going nowhere, and I was in no hurry at the moment. I slid over her slowly, kissing her lightly on her neck, near her shoulder, and then I went across and kissed her more strongly and moved to her breasts again. I took my time. She arched and sighed. She moved and said my name and lightly scratched her fingernails across my back. She was floating, and I touched her belly and thighs, and then I opened her and felt her, moist and warm, and that was where I kissed and put my mouth and kissed more deeply.

Then the urgency took us both. I moved over her, and she opened under me, took me in her hand, and gently and slowly let me inside, into her secrets. She gasped and moaned, and I loved the scent of her skin, which made me crazy with love, lust, want and desire. At that moment, the only thought I had was being thankful I could not see. My world was pure sensation. I felt nothing outside of being entwined and then inside her. There was no other feeling, just that. Just there. It swept over all of me, and I felt on fire.

"Yes! Oh, Jake!" Sophie cried out. She was writhing and moving hard against me and I knew she felt completely free. We began to move in a rhythm that was not smooth but rough and without conscious thought, each of us deep into the other, fucking now more than making love. It was primal and wonderful, and we were both caught up in it. We trusted each other and so were free to do whatever we wanted, and we sighed, cried out, lost each other, and then found each other again with kisses. Then all thought was gone again, and we became physical and greedy and we moved in pure joy. We finished together, kissing, rolling around, and then laughing, and she sobbed a little. I kissed her brow and gently wiped the tears off her face.

There was silence for a few moments and then I startled her by growling like a panther, and went crazy, kissing her all over her face and breasts a hundred times.

We were soon making love again. Slower this time. I went all the way inside her and then stopped and just held myself there, and she clasped her hands around the base of my spine and wouldn't let me out again.

"This is how we will always be," she said. "Always together, no matter what happens."

"No matter what happens," I said. I stayed inside her even after we finished making love the second time, and we fell asleep that way.

The next morning, the moon was gone, and the sun was making its way up, but it didn't matter. We made love again before breakfast. We came, arching. I traced the outline of her face after that, and she laughed. Her laughter sounded like music and I was completely happy.

I have been happy like that several times since then, but it was always with Sophie. Always.

We held hands and acted like lovers all morning, and Sophie whispered to me that people in the café and on the sidewalks were smiling at us.

Of course, no one can see into the future, so people smile at what they see, and sometimes it is good they cannot see into the future.

Chapter 36

I knew Sophie was not fully healed from the war, but our trip had begun the healing process, and there was no hint of sadness in her smile anymore. We laughed, hugged and made love in the night and sometimes in the afternoons. She talked about her parents and was sad sometimes, but we both knew that was natural. She told me she was happy and that's all that mattered to me.

We said our goodbyes to the people who ran the hotel and to the village, and there was no sadness because we knew we could come back, many times.

We had been on the train back to Paris for less than an hour, when I began to experience more light flashes. For seconds at a time, I could actually see sustained light. Sophie was tremendously excited. I was frightened, actually. I didn't know what to expect, and I had to trust her completely. She demanded I tell her exactly what was happening.

"It's like explosions of light, different colors, like bombs, only these are good bombs," I said.

She laughed, but she kept me focused and talking. She reassured me constantly that it was a normal, restorative progression. I nodded, but inside, I was a wreck.

"You are healing! This is how it works!" she said

excitedly. We were sitting alone. At one point she became quiet.

"What?" I said.

"I don't know. What if, when you can see me, you don't like me?" she said. "I am not perfect."

"Did you forget?" I said firmly. "I have seen you! And sadly, no, you are not perfect." I was going to tease her but sensed it wasn't time for that. "Any more than an angel is perfect," I added.

"Thank you," she said softly. "I need to trust you, and I do. We will get used to you seeing again, and we will love each other more than ever."

Then there was another flash of light, and that one did not go away. "I can see light even through these bandages!" I shouted. "Why didn't the doctors tell me this would happen?"

"They did not want you to hope. They are not in the hope business. They are in some other business."

"Bastards," I said.

Sophie laughed. "I will tell them how much you appreciate them."

"Sophie, this scares me. I want to see again, but I don't want anything to happen to us."

"Nothing will happen, except you will make love to me in Paris."

"But you are in love with me?"

"Of course. I will tell you that a million times."

"Oh God," I said.

I saw more light, and now I saw it all the time. It was

yellow and gold, and there were flecks of red and silver – no shapes, but light.

We rode on and the clatter of the tracks was rhythmic. Sophie fell asleep on my shoulder. I leaned my head against her hair as the train bumped and gently rattled its way back to Paris. Throughout the morning, the incredible light – light I'd thought I would never see again – kept streaming in through my bandages. I expected to feel more amazed and excited, but it felt so normal that I had to think back to remember that twenty-four hours before, I had been in constant darkness.

My sight was returning not in some dramatic way, as one might have seen in the cinema, but as Sophie had said it would – gradually and steadily – and I found myself not willing to think of how lucky I was. I had kept the idea that my blindness was temporary as my reality the entire time. The alternative would have overwhelmed me. The irony in my finding Sophie and falling in love with her, when I could not see her, did not occur to me until later. I was just trying to get through each day without going crazy, so it was hard for me to focus on anything else, especially something as complicated as irony. Irony took time, energy, and maybe a little whiskey to fully appreciate. I had other things on my mind.

Late that afternoon, we entered Paris and I was excited about seeing the city again. When the trained slowed and we pulled into the station, I could see light all the time through the bandages. I told Sophie that as the train stopped.

"I know someplace we must go," she said. She wouldn't tell me where.

We gathered our suitcases and she waved down a taxi. The driver laid our things in the trunk and Sophie gave him our destination out of my earshot. She was excited about her surprise.

Finally, the taxi pulled over and we got out. The driver took our suitcases out of the trunk. We paid him and he drove off.

"Now?" I asked impatiently.

"Yes, now," she said.

She took a step behind me and I felt her hands on the knot that tied my bandages. Slowly, she worked the knot loose and then she unwrapped the gauze-like strips from around my head and eyes. As she came to the final one, the light seemed to grow fiercely bright.

"When I take this one off, shut your eyes and put your hands over them and only take them off when you think you can stand the light," she said.

I did what she said, and she unwrapped the last bandage. The light hurt for a few moments, but then it seemed to be okay and I tried opening my eyes just a little. The light hurt too much, and I closed my eyes again. I did that several times and it seemed to get better. By looking down at the ground away from the sun, I found I could keep my eyes open for seconds at a time and then longer moments, until finally, I could keep them open without too much pain.

"Are you ready?" Sophie asked. "Can you stand to look up?"

I nodded.

She turned me around and I looked up and saw the Cathedral de Notre-Dame. Its splendid walls and spires rose up toward heaven and the gargoyles stared down at me. This time, it seemed to me they were grinning. It was a church of sight, a gift from Sophie, the shaman.

"I love you," I said.

Strangely, Sophie did not say anything. Though she was blurry still, I could see her clearly enough and she was staring at me with a bad look on her face. She caught herself and moved toward me – but with some effort, it appeared. What was wrong? I felt panic. She moved in and hugged me for a long time under the walls of the cathedral, but the joy I had felt a moment ago vanished. I caught a look on her face that she tried to hide. It looked like dismay. I wanted with all my heart to believe it was because she was seeing my eyes for the first time. Maybe they were reddened by the bandages.

"We must go back to my apartment," she said.

"I thought we would have lunch here," I said.

"No!" she said with a sharpness that surprised me.

"Okay," I said.

She quickly waved over another cab and we rode back to her apartment. The cab driver said little to us. He looked at me in a funny way, but I was wild about seeing the images around me, which were still a little blurry but becoming clearer by the moment.

We walked, and I tried to see everything at once, but it made me a little dizzy and I simply followed Sophie.

"I live there." She pointed to the second story of a neat, clean building that had balconies overlooking the street and then much of Paris.

I took both suitcases.

"There is no lift," Sophie said.

"That's okay, I can lift it all!" I said, hoisting the suitcases up.

She smiled briefly – too briefly I thought – and led the way to the side of the building, where large stone stairs led up to the front door of her second-story apartment. I was ecstatic as we climbed the stairs, as though the world were ours' – Sophie's and mine.

More than anything, I wanted to make love to her again, and I was crazy with the idea by the time we got to the top of the stairs. She produced a large key and unlocked the door. She went inside ahead of me. I followed quickly. The living room was small, neat, and clean. It was also clearly feminine, with lace and delicate things on the end tables and armoire. It was the kind of room most men appreciated but could not duplicate. I was about to take the suitcases past the door that I thought led to the bedroom, when Sophie stopped me.

"Oh, Jake, there is something…"

Before she could say anything else, I swept her off her feet and held her in my arms. I walked quickly to the bedroom door and pushed it open with my foot.

"Jake, no, no!" she screamed. "Wait."

I almost dropped her when I saw. There was a huge, beautiful mirror on one side of her bedroom. In it, I saw my own face – or what had been my face – and what was left of my face. I couldn't think, I couldn't even feel for a moment. A large, ugly, red-flamed scar ran down across my forehead and across my eye to my cheek. I didn't know the man in the mirror looking back at me. The man I was looking at was terrified, horrified and disfigured. I took a step forward and shuddered from head to toe in denial.

That wasn't me!

It was a monster.

I fell to my knees in horror.

Sophie stood for a moment with her hands covering her mouth, unable to move. Then she rushed toward me, shouting things I couldn't hear. All I could do was stare at the scarred man. Maybe he would disappear and I would appear, I thought, but a cold fist clenched my heart. It was me. Then a demon rose up and took over.

I brushed Sophie aside and raced out the door and down the stairs. I ignored her shouted pleas behind me. I ran down the streets, across the boulevards, and through the parks, past the staring people. The demon took over, and I let it. I ran and ran and ran.

Late that night, I reached the hotel where Margaret and I had checked in so many lifetimes ago. The fat doorman was there, and he looked at me when I stumbled in looking disheveled, as though I had seen a ghost, or perhaps I was the ghost.

"*Bonsoir monsieur*," he said, acting as though nothing were out of the ordinary. "If you are wondering, the mademoiselle is gone, but the room is available for you," he said. I knew he was talking about Margaret. "If I may say so, sir, *bon debarras!* You are most welcome."

I didn't know whether he was greeting me or assumed I was going to thank him for his comment about Margaret, but either way, I didn't care. My focus had narrowed to one thing, and one thing only. I would find the little thief who'd ruined my life, and I would kill him.

Chapter 37

There is a trend in modern science to believe that madness is inherited, but if that is true, then it must be inherited at one time or another by just about everyone in the human race. Everyone, sooner or later, goes at least a little mad – some of us more than a little.

On a statue in a Parisian gallery are words that could have proven my own epitaph had things turned out differently. "Man is certainly stark mad. He can't make a worm, yet he makes gods by the dozens." For the next three days and nights after I left Sophie, I was definitely stark, crazy mad.

Someone told me that often we don't know we have gone mad until later, when we are no longer mad, and then we look back and marvel and shrink in wonder of how that could have been. I am not sure that is true. I was aware that I was out of control, but I was so frustrated and lost I didn't care. I prowled and hunted in the streets of Paris. I hunted for the man who had struck me down and made a furrow, as straight and as true as a corn row, across my face and my soul. I did not carry a weapon. I wanted to complete my revenge with my bare hands. I refused to think about Sophie. How could I? I was as imperfect as a man could have been. There was only one thing left to do.

I ate little and slept less during that time. I stayed away from mirrors, but I knew I looked as gruesome as the gargoyles. Maybe they would put me up on the side of the cathedral when they caught me. I told myself that grim joke many times as I haunted the dark streets of Paris.

I jammed my fists into my jacket and said little to anyone, and always, I was looking for the thief. Several times during the days, I saw a profile like his, but when I hurried to catch up, each time with blood roiling up in my veins, I found it wasn't him. At night I stalked the riverfront, especially on the docks where he'd tried to rob me. Sometimes I even slept there, hidden away behind the crates and pallets, covered only with my jacket. I did not want to be comfortable because that would have meant a deeper sleep, and I did not want to miss my fierce revenge. I ate sparingly – an apple or maybe a croissant from the bakeries – and I saw discomfort in people's faces when they looked at me. They usually put their heads down and avoided me, and I wanted it that way. There was only one person on earth who interested me – and I wanted to kill him.

Late on the second day, I finally went back to my hotel room, knowing I risked arrest if I slept on the streets again. The doorman just stared at me when I came in, and then he shook his head and walked away. When I got to my door, I saw it was covered in papers, pinned with small tacks. They were notes, all in Sophie's handwriting. In the notes, she pleaded with me to stop my hunting and come back. I crumpled them and tossed them into the dark, unlit fireplace. I had no dreams that afternoon as I slept. There seemed to be no dreams left.

It was already dark, and I was still sleeping when Robert knocked on my door. He had two men with him when I opened it a crack and squinted out. I recognized Jean-Claude, the police inspector, and the bulky dark form behind him I recognized as the writer. I was embarrassed and annoyed.

"What do you want?" I asked.

"We are concerned, Jake. What the hell is going on?" said Robert.

"Nothing. I cannot talk to you, now." I tried to shut the door.

"I am sorry, Jake," said the Inspector, stepping forward and putting the toe of his shoe against the door so I couldn't shut it. "We've had reports, and we want to make sure you are okay."

"Reports? No. Go to hell. Go away."

The Inspector leaned his shoulder against the door and pushed his way in. I must have let him because I was much stronger than he was. I also felt guilty about telling him to go to hell.

All three men strode into the room. The writer sported a large smile. He was enjoying the drama playing out in front of him.

Robert closed on me and grasped my shoulders. I noticed that his gaze went immediately to the gash on my forehead. It seemed to take effort for him to re-focus on me. "Jesus, Jake, what the hell is happening to you? You have regained your eyesight, man! It's a damn miracle. Why aren't you out celebrating? Have a glass of wine with us, and then there is a special lady waiting for you. Come on!"

I said nothing but shook my head slightly.

Robert frowned.

Jean-Claude also frowned. He stood with his arms crossed. He was giving me a posture of caring authority. I scowled. I wanted to stand and roar and frighten them, but the concern on Robert's face was so real that the madness passed quickly, and I suddenly felt weary and sat down on the couch. The writer still had a wide grin. I should have been angriest at him, but somehow, his grin pierced through my anger. He knew well what it was like to go mad and he did not disapprove. I also knew instinctively that he was amused by the fact that he knew it was my first time.

He had said nothing, but he and I communicated the most.

"Come with us to the hospital, and we'll have you checked out and get a dressing back on your head," Robert said. "It's bleeding some. Did you even know that? Jesus, Jake, what are you doing?"

"You should come with us," Jean-Claude added.

"I am fine. I don't need a hospital."

The Inspector stepped forward as if to force me to get up and go with them, but the writer stopped him.

"Gentlemen, let us go to the bar and have champagne or beer or whiskey, but let us leave this man alone. He is not coming with us. Madness has its own timetable."

Jean-Claude hesitated, as if not sure what his duty was, but Robert nodded.

"Call me tomorrow, or we are coming back," he said to me.

I nodded slightly, and they left.

I turned the lights off and sat in the darkness for a long time before I fell asleep on the couch.

The next day, I felt no different. It was dark, cloudy and windy outside, and I walked the streets again. I did not eat breakfast or lunch and walked down rue Mouffetard, oblivious to the powerful scents of new bread, sliced oranges and crepes being prepared in the cafés. I didn't care about food or anything else. Everything I once had held as true was gone. The gods had taken my beliefs, Margaret had taken my trust, and the little thief had taken my dreams. I was a dangerous man with nothing to lose.

By late afternoon I reached the docks and slipped into my hiding place behind the thick apple crates. I could see the entire dock from where I was, but no one could see me. There was only one man, though, who needed to fear me.

Two hours after sunset, darkness had fallen, but there were still a few straggling tourists walking the banks of the river to watch the moon rise over the water. That was when I saw him. He appeared like a shadow, moving almost unseen across the dock. I tensed, and then the rage came back in full force, and I had to fight myself not to rush out at him. I knew he was exceptionally smart and agile, and my revenge depended on stealth first, and then strength and savageness. He was stalking two people who looked like Americans. The man's coat bulged where a wallet was obviously stuffed in a pocket, and the woman's purse carelessly dangled off her shoulder. They were easy prey. Except this time was different. This time he was the prey. He just didn't yet know it.

The two Americans could not see me but angled toward my hiding place so they could get past the storage buildings and look at the shattered light of the rising moon reflecting off the river currents. As they were walking past me, the woman suddenly became animated about something and grabbed the man's arm. She talked excitedly for a moment, the man nodded, and they turned abruptly and walked back the way they had come. I assumed she had forgotten a coat or an appointment of some type. Whatever it was, it left the thief and me momentarily alone on the dock. He watched them and seemed unsure of what to do. He stood like a dark soldier about twenty yards from me.

That was when I attacked.

I burst out of my hiding place like an avenging ghost. He didn't react at first, but then his feral instincts kicked in. He dodged at the last moment and I managed only a glancing blow to his temple as I went by. He reeled but stayed on his feet. Backing up, he quickly realized he had nowhere to go. I had him trapped by the edge of the dock. He had to fight or jump into the river, which swirled like a black snake ten feet below. He chose to fight and went into a crouch, with his fists up. I could see he was frightened.

"Go! Please go! I have nothing!" he shouted in French.

I ignored him and closed in again. He tried a feint to my left – a mistake. As he moved back to my right, I stepped forward and hit him as hard as I could. My fist crashed into his chin, with rage behind it, and he went limp. He was unconscious even before he fell. He tilted backward as straight as a board and for a moment, his falling body was silhouetted against the moonlit water. Then he disappeared. A moment later, I heard the splash.

Chapter 38

For an instant, I felt insanely, wildly triumphant. My revenge was complete. I had vanquished my enemy who had destroyed me. But then, as suddenly as it had come on, the madness left my body like a demon fleeing in the darkness. I stepped to the edge of the dock and saw the little thief's body floating downstream facedown.

I had been trying to kill him for three days. Now there he was. He was sinking even as I watched. He would likely be dead in a few moments. Then I heard someone screaming.

I turned and saw no one, but the shouting became so loud I wanted to cover my ears. Then I realized it was me, shouting at myself to pull him out of the water. I knew I had to try to save him. Or maybe I knew I had to try to save myself.

I ripped off my jacket and shoes and dove into the black water. The coldness of the river was shocking, and the power of the current was such that I came up fifteen feet from where I had gone in. I could not see him. I swam hard. With the current shoving me along, it was like being lashed to the front of a race car. The moon glittered across the surface, and I realized I was covering too much ground. I might have gone past him. I turned to fight the current, but it nearly flipped me over. I raised myself up above the water as high as I could and paddled around in a circle, shouting as I did. He was not on top of the water. I took a deep breath and dove. It was truly black down there. Even the moon couldn't get through the swift waters, but strangely, I felt at home. I had been in total darkness for most of the past few months, and I did not panic.

I kicked and swam forward hard, waving my arms in all directions, trying to find him. My hand brushed something, and I grabbed it and pulled. Then I rammed into his body. I had his shirt in my fist. It was a solid hold, and I instantly kicked with all my strength for the surface. The current was cunningly strong, though, and it pulled us back down and under and farther down.

Now I felt like panicking. Then I thought I saw the moon, and, in its light, I saw my father's face, I saw the clouds, and I saw the gods. They all seemed to look at me for a long moment and then, all at once, they faded away into the darkness. It was a moment of total freedom.

With renewed strength, I held on to the little thief and kicked again hard toward the surface. I still had air in my lungs, and I still had fight. I kicked and pulled with my other hand, and I did not stop until we broke the surface. We shot up above the current, so our chests were out, and I gasped for air, and it came into my lungs. The thief was limp. His chin hung down over my arm. I angled us downstream, and I was mostly under him, holding his head above the water as much as I could. Then I made out the bulk of the shoreline about twenty yards away. I strengthened my grip on him and then stretched out for the shore. The river was far from done with us, though.

The currents collided at one point and pulled us down,

and we went under again. It seemed to happen in slow motion, and we spun slowly around. I saw Sophie's face, it seemed as if she smiled at me, and then we came up slowly, and I did not let go, nor did we go under again. I swam for a long time, it seemed, and we edged toward the shore. I felt my strength was good as we neared the bank, but when it became more visible, my heart froze. It was steep, far too steep for me to get him out. There were no branches or handholds, and I realized we were in trouble.

The eddy was strong near the shore and threatened to swing us around out into the middle of the river again. I spread my free arm out toward the bank and tried to grab anything I could, but there was nothing. I had not given up, but I was gasping for air, when a big arm and a human hand came down from the top of the bank and grabbed the little thief by the back of his shirt collar. He was hoisted up by someone with astonishing strength right out of the water. I was startled, gulped a mouthful of water, and was sucked back from the bank, and pulled under again by the current. Without the burden of the thief, though, it was easier, and I kicked up and out of the river, and onto the muddy bank.

After a long moment of catching my breath, I pulled myself the rest of the way out of the river and lay exhausted in the grass on the bank. I could see a dark form on the ground. The little thief was lying there breathing – slightly and irregularly, but he was breathing. I was glad then that he was a tough son of a bitch. I turned him onto his side, and soon he began to fidget and move. Then his chest erupted, and he coughed out quantities of black water from his lungs. Finally, his eyes opened, and they looked right into mine.

"Am I in hell?" he asked in a heavy accent.

I couldn't help but laugh. "No," I said. "But we were close."

He lay there and then as though he remembered where he was and how he'd gotten there, he pulled back away from me.

"What are you going to do?" he asked, his eyes darting for a weapon.

"Easy," I said. "I hit you, but I also pulled you out. I could have left you in the river."

He eyed me warily, but neither of us moved.

Finally, I pointed to the gash on my face. "Remember this?"

He flinched slightly.

"Yeah, you remember," I said. "You are a son of a bitch!"

He looked at me, frowned, and stuck his chin out. "You are *un fils de pute*" he said. He tried to snarl when he said it, but it was a lousy snarl. To make up for it, he indignantly pointed to his leg, which had a deep gash and was bleeding where he must have scraped it against a sunken tree branch. He also touched his chin, which was already showing a fine purple bump, like a small plum. "*Un fils de pute*," he said again softly, almost like a child.

I shook my head. We both knew the fighting was over. He was still groggy and in no shape to run, fight or do anything other than trust me anyway. Still watching me carefully, he said his name was Emile, and I told him mine. It was an odd moment, but somehow, as we lay side by side and soaking wet on the dark riverbank, it seemed to make some kind of sense, and we did not question it.

I tore off a piece of his shirt and wrapped it around his leg. "I know you do not want to go to a hospital. I will take you to where you live. You need attention to that leg."

He raised his hand and I yanked him up, making sure he could lean against me to take the pressure off his leg. We walked together up the quay. The taxi driver I hailed merely shrugged as though it weren't unusual to pick up two wet and bloody men from the river. He drove us across the bridge and into the city until the little thief told him to stop, and he did. I made the thief pay him with soggy money he pulled from his pants pocket. The driver held up the dripping bills with his thumb and forefinger, shrugged, and drove away.

We managed to get down a pathway I would not have seen, down under the bridge, through the hidden doorway, and into the cave, which was lit with a hundred candles. It was the overwhelmingly delightful scent of a fresh dinner that attracted me the most.

The black dog came running up, licked the man's hand, and then he licked mine and jumped around wagging his tail. The walls were beautifully polished stone, and the hideout had different levels, with each offering something new – including a sitting room, and a big, open kitchen with big pots and kettles and a huge wooden dining table. Tall beautiful doors blocked openings to other parts of the cavernous underground, and there were many children, men and women. They all seemed at peace with each other. A huge fireplace gave everything a warm orange light. It was the weirdest thing I had ever seen.

In a moment, we were surrounded by nearly everyone in the room. They crowded in, and questions came from all directions. An attractive woman with dark hair and keen, intelligent eyes scrutinized me as she cleaned and bandaged the cut on Emile's leg. I knew I had seen her before.

Chapter 39

Emile was clearly a man of importance in that place. The others treated him with great respect, and they all wanted to know what had happened. He was the prince of thieves. I was the man who'd saved him. They didn't care that I was also the one who'd knocked him into the river in the first place. I had saved him, and he was pleased and honored by what I had done. He told the story, leaving out certain parts, including how he had robbed me and how I had hunted him down. He said only that I had fished him out of the deadly current. They seemed happy with the story.

A hot cup of tea and a plate of dinner appeared, and they waited patiently while I drank the tea and cleaned the plate. The food was delicious; orange and sweet plums and thin slices of meat. A glass of dark Bordeaux appeared, and I toasted them all and drank. The feeling in the room was joyous and friendly. They sat and drank and waited for me. They refused to move away from me until I said something. I told them I was from America, from the middle part, where the food grew and it got cold in the winter and hot in the summer. I said I wanted to be a decent writer someday, and they nodded and said they thought I would be. They poured more wine, and then two guitars were produced and some songs burst out. They all sang and drank more wine. The flames rose high in the fireplace, and the black dog, his coat hot on the side facing the fire, staked a claim on my feet, curled up and fell asleep.

Then, Emile's wife, Bridgette, was beside me. "You know, we have met before," she said in a low voice. Of course I remembered.

"You were in a hurry and you almost knocked me down."

"Yes, and I was sorry for that."

"Yes, so you said."

"You called me a gangster." I looked around and laughed. "That seems very funny now. Who is the gangster?"

She laughed lightly. "We are all gangsters in one way or another. Thank you for saving Emile. I know there is much more to the story than either of you is admitting, but I will leave it alone. The story is very good just as it is now."

Then she gently touched the wound on my forehead. I had forgotten about it until then. I shrank back. "It is ugly," I said before I realized I was going to say anything.

"No!" Bridgette said swiftly. "Do not think that!" Then she disappeared for a moment, returned with a cup, and scooped a clear salve-like substance out of it. She smoothed it onto my forehead, and she rubbed it carefully into my skin and around the wound. "This wound will heal, and the scar will fade, but it will take time. But something else might not. If you are going to be a decent writer, you must know something." She stopped and stared into my eyes, and I could not look away.

"You fear imperfection. But there is no such thing as a perfect place, a perfect world, or a perfect love." Then she looked across at her husband, who had been listening, and she smiled. "A beautiful love, yes! We can achieve that. And that is even better."

She looked back at me.

"A woman once told me there is no perfect in art or love," I said. "I didn't know what she meant until tonight."

"Ah, and where is that woman now?" Bridgette asked with raised eyebrows.

I stared at her. I stood up suddenly, knocking the chair over behind me. The black dog woke up and everyone in the room stopped and looked.

"I have to go!" I shouted in English. I hugged Bridgette, shook Emile's hand quickly, yelled *"Merci!"* and *"Au revoir!"* many times, and ran out the door as fast as I could.

They yelled back and kept singing.

Outside, it was cold. My clothes were still wet from the river. The freezing wind felt like a whip. It had blown clouds over the moon. It was dark, but my footing was good, and I made it to the street above. There were no taxis in sight, so I began to run. I ran up the Quai Montebello and down Boulevard Saint-Germain and cut across a small park. The moon came out for a moment, low in the sky to my right. An owl banked against the soft lining of silver moonlight, and then I heard a girl's voice singing clearly and beautifully. She sang in French and I did not know what she was singing, but it gave me great energy.

As I raced through the city, the sky closed, and it began to rain again. I had to wipe my eyes as I ran. My shoes splashed on the sidewalk. I turned a final corner and saw the light in her apartment. It was the most beautiful and brightest light in the universe.

"Sophie!" I shouted. It didn't sound like my voice, and I wasn't sure I had even made a noise. The rain went into my eyes and I blinked, but I didn't stop looking up at the window and the magic light. Then I saw her silhouette and saw her move, and she came to the window and slightly parted the curtain. She looked out across the rooftops and then down to the street and saw me. She put her hands up, turned away and left the window.

I shouted again, ran to the stairs and leaped up them, three at a time. My heart pounded. By the time I reached the top, her door was already open.

Epilogue

A month later, on a warm day in June, I met the writer on a grassy bank of the river. Through Robert, I had asked for the meeting. I was surprised he'd agreed, but I had to know. He appeared early in the afternoon, feeling fine because he had had a morning of good writing. He held a sack full of oranges and chestnuts. I did not ask what he was writing and he did not tell me.

"Hello," I said.

He didn't say anything at first. He just looked at me and shook his big, shaggy head. "Why aren't you writing?" he asked finally.

I laughed. I had no answer. He didn't laugh. Instead, he said, "What you wrote in the magazine was not horrible."

I knew that was as big a compliment as I was going to get from him. I nodded, but only slightly.

"If one believes in muses, one might be tempted to say they are all on vacation in Paris, France," he said. "Currently, no place on earth has a greater gathering of artists than the City of Light. They drink, carouse and are as self-centered as young children sometimes, but the world will long remember and admire what is being done there."

I was stunned. He had memorized much of I had written in the magazine.

"Don't be flattered," he said. "It wasn't all good, what you wrote, but that part was true, and I saw it. But there is far more that is true, and there is far more that you should write, although don't try to write as well as I do, or you will stop."

He laughed.

I looked at him. "Did you help us that night on the riverbank?"

The writer looked out over the swirling current. "Sometimes I take walks at night. But you need to remember the only stories that are any good are the ones that come from your imagination. But sometimes they are true."

As usual, I didn't know exactly what he meant, but I knew enough. He was not a god but a finely complicated man – a rogue, a bastard, a genius and a possible friend.

We were silent for moment, and then he turned to me.

"You wanted something from me in our interview," he said. "Here it is. You should write for two people. Yourself, to make it absolutely perfect or if not that, then wonderful. Then you should write for the one you love, whether they can read or write or not, or whether they are alive or dead."

I could not have known then how prophetic his words would prove to be.

He slapped me on the back, smiled slightly, walked to the bridge and crossed over the river. It was not the last time I would see him in Paris.

In the end, although Sophie and I had dinner with Robert, Allison and Inspector Jean-Claude many times, I never told them about the incident at the river or about the cave. I debated it – they were thieves after all – but somehow, I could not bring myself to do it.

Sophie and I saw them occasionally and we smiled. Once I even saw Emile and his black dog, although they didn't see me. Cassie came regularly to visit, and we went out to the cafés, where we talked and laughed while the doves angled across the rooftops.

I loved Sophie fiercely and she loved me back. I held her hand a great deal on the boulevards. Paris was always there for us after that. We saw it clearly every morning from her balcony.